T0121100

SOw RIGHT

(Re)Discovering Purposeful Living

d.w. freeman

WESTBOW
PRESS®
A DIVISION OF THOMAS NELSON
& ZONDERVAN

WestBow Press books may be ordered through
booksellers or by contacting:

WestBow Press
A Division of Thomas Nelson & Zondervan
1663 Liberty Drive
Bloomington, IN 47403
www.westbowpress.com
844-714-3454

Scripture quotations taken from The Holy Bible, New International
Version® NIV® Copyright © 1973 1978 1984 2011 by Biblica, Inc.
TM. Used by permission. All rights reserved worldwide.

ISBN: 978-1-6642-4444-3 (sc)
ISBN: 978-1-6642-4446-7 (hc)
ISBN: 978-1-6642-4445-0 (e)

Library of Congress Control Number: 2021918298

Print information available on the last page.

WestBow Press rev. date: 9/24/2021

CONTENTS

People: The world is full of us. We are so alike yet so different. We have individual backgrounds, beliefs, and paths yet one thing in common, a desire to live a life fulfilled with purpose.

The quest for purpose hinges on beliefs. Do you have definitive beliefs of who you are? Do you have definitive beliefs of who God is or isn't? How do your beliefs affect the way you live?

This book is intended to help define beliefs about yourself, God, and strengths needed for a fulfilled, purposeful life. It is meant to stimulate personal growth through insight of God's desire for you.

It starts with guidance on defining one's self: who you see yourself as and what you rely upon to shape your identity. This "search of self" leads to defining your belief in God and how his presence relates to purpose and fulfillment. The last section provides insight into God's instruction for personal traits that support the pursuit of living with purpose and fulfillment.

The material in this book has been used to lead discussions with Christians and non-Christians alike, from high schoolers to middle-aged persons. Hopefully it will help regardless of age, religion, or relationship with God. There are no suppositions that you have checked the box on church attendance or are a non-, new, or old Christian. The only requirement is to have the courage to examine yourself, your belief in God, and your faith in God's presence.

This book considers the Bible to be the most authoritative source of written communication from and about God. As such, scriptural references are provided throughout the topics. They are referenced from the New International

Version (NIV) translation. Readers are encouraged to seek additional scripture that relate to the subject as well as seek other translations of the noted scripture. And most importantly, read passages before and after the listed verses to obtain clarity from the context of the surrounding text.

PART I
SOw WHAT ABOUT ME

We all desire to live with a sense of purpose and fulfillment. It starts with a sense of who you are and why you are alive. These beliefs direct us through the countless "who, what, where, when, and how" questions of our daily life. You may believe God's authority, nature's control, self-empowerment, random chance, or any number of entities lead you through life. Regardless, it starts with your perceptions about your own abilities and desires.

The ancient Greeks are credited with the phrase "Know Thyself." William Shakespeare added purpose to this philosophy with the phrase, "This above all: to thine own self be true, And it must follow, as the night the day, Thou canst not then be false to any man" (*Hamlet* Act 1, scene 3). It's good advice to start a journey. Unfortunately many of us have not clearly defined our thoughts about who we really are to be true "to thine own self." So we develop routines to avoid the question of what we believe to be true and what we hold as essential parts of our identity.

Part I: SOw What About Me is intended to help define who you are and how others perceive you. Maybe you are just starting out in this pursuit, have just gone through a life-changing experience that has you questioning your previous thoughts of purpose and fulfillment, have grown to the point of feeling you have reached the end of that pursuit, or have been so confused about life in general that you don't feel capable of pursuit.

Here's some profound advice: Start with a starting point. Well, that advice doesn't sound so profound after all. Maybe you can come up with something better. No doubt, motivational speakers can say it better. How about "every journey begins with the courage to take the first step"?

The approach taken in this book is that you, the individual, is the starting point for taking that first step of the journey to finding purpose and meaning of being alive. Clarifying your thoughts of who you believe yourself to be will give you the stability and courage to focus on the challenge of pursuing where you want to go. Ready? Let's get started.

🌱 1
JUST WHAT DO I STAND FOR?

❧ A SHORT FICTIONAL STORY

They found themselves standing next to one another while waiting for the subway. Strangers who were more different wasn't possible: a young gang member, a well-to-do businessman, and a man of the cloth. Uneasy thoughts were conveyed without words. The young man was trying to not show he was nervous so to avoid suspicion. The last thing he wanted was to be hassled. To him, it was just the same old story of misunderstood youth versus the establishment.

The businessman's fear was evidenced only by his quick glance toward the young man and the priest. He stood exactly halfway between them so to be out of reach. His thoughts of judgment fell on the boy, obviously just another kid who was worthless, lazy, and likely a thief—if not something worse. To him, that was what was wrong with this world. Young people just don't care about anything other than themselves, always wanting the easy way out of the responsibility of life.

And then there was the priest, consumed with his

list of duties that served as evidence and justification of goodness. It was all he could do to remember where he was going next. Was it the hospital? No, that wasn't it. Oh yes, lunch with a civic club to share all the church was doing to improve the neighborhood. His only contact with the other two was a quick glance at the businessman. Was he a member of his church? Hopefully not. He was just too preoccupied to act like he was happy to see anyone.

In an instant, their stationary moment evolved into chaos. Something grabbed their attention. A young mother was sitting on a bench, engrossed in the screen of her phone. Her toddler took off and in an instant was on the edge of the track. Then just as quickly, the child was out of sight, falling onto the tracks at the exact time of the approaching train.

The priest was frozen. All he could muster were thoughts of another senseless tragedy. The businessman's first thought was to turn away. Neither saw the young man. He wasn't standing by them. He had jumped down to the tracks and in one motion grabbed and threw the child back up on the standing area. The child was unharmed. The young man wasn't so lucky.

~ PRINCIPLES

The story is based upon a parable in Luke 10. It is not meant to bash the inactions of the priest or businessman or the inattentiveness of the mother or to emphasize the fragility of life. It is meant to demonstrate how one's beliefs guide one's actions and how actions define beliefs.

All of us live by standards of ethics, morality, and character. Our principles (tenets and doctrine), whether based on truth or not, serve as the foundation for our actions. These are the standards we have decided to be the most consistent, firmly grounded, important rules for shaping our thoughts, making decisions, and guiding actions. As such, these principles shape our identity.

We think and act in ways that demonstrate these beliefs, be they good or bad, socially acceptable or unacceptable, selfish or selfless, or right or wrong. We form thoughts about our purpose for living from our principles, and we gain fulfillment when we sense we are accomplishing that purpose. When we are so thoroughly convinced that something is absolutely true, we take a stand for it regardless of the consequences. Our principles then become our convictions. And it is these convictions that drive us to living with purpose and fulfilment.

At first thought, the idea of acting on our principles might be restricted to times requiring life-altering decisions or times of great crisis. However, beliefs are demonstrated most often during the frequency of daily routine and, as most of us live with some level of prosperity, during the good times as often as the bad.

❧ PRINCIPLES PERSONIFIED

Think about someone in your past who made a positive impact on your life. List the reasons you believe the person was so influential. Likely, your list has items that refer to both the person's aptitude and attitude. Are your reasons related to what you believe the person's values were?

I think of my senior year high school English teacher, Mrs. Dancy. She was finishing a lifelong career as a high school teacher. She wasn't only old; she was old school:

diagraming sentences, conjugating verbs, and requiring us to recite Shakespeare by memory, stuff you would think high school seniors of the 1970s would rebel against. After all, this was a time of sit-ins, rebellion, nonconformity, and individuality.

But we didn't rebel in her classroom. Somehow her belief in us and our belief in her transcended everything else. We were obedient because we respected the value of the instructor. We were open to learning because of our belief in the instructor. We believed she cared about her craft and, more importantly, us. We had faith that what she taught was more valuable than our understanding of its value at the time. We believed this because of our faith in who she was and what she stood for. And I still think about her with feelings of thanks.

Hopefully, you've concluded like I have that all of us live by principles and that these tenets form the basis of identity and thoughts on the purpose for living. For principles to be valuable, they must be real. In order to be real, they must be based on truth. If true, they must be demonstrated by our actions consistently during times of abundance, routine, and crisis.

Can you think of one or two tenets that you heavily rely upon for shaping your identity? Do you believe honesty is important? Maybe you are driven by the urge to respond to a particular type of social injustice. Perhaps it's in the pursuit of knowledge in some technical field for the betterment of future generations. Maybe it isn't so socially positive, such as "get ahead by any means necessary" or "survival of the fittest and death to the weak."

Just what do you value and rely upon to set your identity? These traits, even though many live under the illusion that they don't, define what you believe about yourself. Your beliefs guide your actions. And your actions shape what others believe about you. The source of these beliefs says a lot about who you are.

∼❧ SHAPING YOUR PRINCIPLES

Your sense of purpose and desire for fulfillment shape the principles you choose to live by. You have the free will to choose your principles and reaction to what life deals you. That may be a bold statement for some, but consequences aside, it is the truth.

For example, your level of financial wealth will not decide your principles. You must decide how wealth governs your thoughts and actions. Think of the stereotypical wealthy people who end life with regret and emptiness for not having lived a purpose-driven life founded on truth. Conversely, some of the strongest and most principled, purpose-driven people who live life fulfilled have little financial wealth.

A variety of influences shape your principles. You have certain genetic tendencies that shape your personality. These traits influence your way of thinking, your desire to socialize, and how you react to circumstances. Your environment modifies these genetically driven tendencies.

Those living with stable authority figures who consistently share their interest, faith, and love may be encouraged more so to act upon their principles. Those blessed with the security of food, shelter, and personal care may have more opportunities to act on their principles. Contrarily, abundance and comfort leading to a sense of self-importance may lead to hopelessness and abandonment of principles.

Hunger, sickness, insecurity, ignorance, fear, danger, and death may push one to establish principles on falsehoods. Feelings of futility, loneliness, and worthlessness are all too common, even in times of abundance and safety. No wonder when considering how easily short-term social norms based on false premises influence us. Even efforts to do good works can be unfulfilling when motives are based on selfishness or falsehood.

CHRISTIAN BELIEF

Defined simply, Christians are followers of Jesus. Followers of Jesus acknowledge that God exists and is the authority of our lives. Followers of Jesus believe Jesus to be God manifested to minister while he was alive on earth. Christians believe Jesus is the anointed one, Christ, and believe his death and resurrection allow forgiveness of sins. Jesus saved us from eternal death. He gave us eternal life. Our salvation allows us a relationship with a holy God and a desire to glorify God.

Salvation is the beginning of a purpose-driven life founded on truth. Christians live governed by God's authority with a love-fueled desire to do as Jesus did, to live to serve God's purpose for humanity.

CHRISTIAN PRINCIPLES

That leads to an introduction, or review, of Christian principles. The core of Christian principles stands on the acceptance that God is in charge and the source of truth. He is alive and active in our lives. We look upon the love, life, death, and resurrection of Jesus as gifts that allow a relationship with God. And we live an empowered life guided by the Holy Spirit.

Christians desire to live in ways that honor and please God. Our sense of worth is heightened when we sense that our efforts please God. Our sense of purpose and good works is most fulfilling when we sense them to be fruitful, worthy, and pleasing to God. Paul explains this in Colossians 1.

Being led by God requires wisdom given by the knowledge and understanding of his will. Relying on God by having faith in his desire for us positions us toward desiring to understand more about him. Pursuing his will shapes our sense of purpose, redefines our principles, and provides a sense of fulfillment. In essence, when we accept and follow his truth, we discover our intended identity and purpose. We live fulfilled when we sense God's love, approval, and blessings.

Seeking God and living out his purpose are universal desires of those who truly follow Jesus. We gain a sense of value that is real and eternal when we accept his tenets as the foundation of our identity. That sense of value gives a sense of true fulfillment unattainable by any other means.

Jesus provides the avenue for discovery of our identity. Accepting Jesus as our Savior doesn't mean we are at the end of the journey to purpose and fulfillment. Rather it opens the door of empowerment to grow toward living purposely. Christians aren't insulated from injustice, pain, sin, and failure. As we are imperfect and live in an imperfect world, we will encounter disappointment even in times of our best intentions and efforts. We will sense futility, doubt, and emptiness at times. We rely on our faith in God's authority, power, mercy, and love to overcome those times of doubt. While disappointments are inevitable, we rely on his power to not be discouraged when they come.

∿ GUIDED BY THE WORD

Christians believe God provided the Bible as his word to mankind. If you are not a Christian, I encourage you to begin to read the Bible at the very least as a book of instruction. Look upon the Bible as a source of what God desires for you personally and all of mankind. Not only read it, but meditate on its message and how the message can apply to your life. Look upon the Bible from the viewpoint of what God wants for you, not from what you want from God. Even though you may not have acknowledged the source, you will likely find that you identify with his instruction.

Seeing the Bible as a source of knowledge about God will position you to understand more about his character and principles. At first, you may think that God's instruction is meant to keep you from experiencing life or to restrict your freedom. Over time, you will feel the opposite if you are earnest and willing to receive his instruction.

This transformation happens as views on purpose and fulfillment change from self-centeredness to a desire to be aligned with God's intent for you. Paul writes about this change of position in Philippians 3.

If you have never read the Bible, you might start with the book of Proverbs in the Old Testament, a record of instruction written many years before the birth of Christ.

Also read the books of the New Testament: Matthew, Mark, Luke, and John. You will find them to be chronicles of Christ's life on earth, with many similar accounts from slightly different perspectives of the individual disciples.

As you read, you will find relatable principles that arise from belief in Christ Jesus. Several possibilities are provided in the following list. These are not all-inclusive or necessarily more important than others you will discover. Each example is paraphrased from scripture with one place of biblical reference.

> Worship God by belief and action above everything else. (Mark 12:28–30)
> Respect all people. (Mark 12:31)
> Be honest. (Luke 16:10)
> Be generous with talents and money. (Matthew 25:34–45)
> Don't hold a grudge. (Matthew 5:43–45)
> Don't be self-righteous. (Matthew 7:1–5)
> Practice what you preach. (Matthew 23:27–28)
> Forgive others. (Matthew 6:14–15)

If you do not consider yourself a Christian, do your beliefs relate to any of the paraphrased tenants? If you are a follower of Jesus, do your actions support these principles? Is there one that is especially meaningful or challenging? Do other verses of instruction come to mind?

❧ DESIRING EXCELLENCE

Each of us must decide on which authorities we allow to guide our actions and shape our beliefs. Most of us, most of the time, allow others to set limits on acceptable behaviors and social norms. We in the United States have laws that govern society differently from other countries. We also have different social influences. There is an inherent danger of measuring the validity and worth of our principles on the legality, norm, or acceptability of society.

The danger in doing so lies with the intended purpose of societal rule. Rules that govern people groups are not meant to define personal principles or purpose, or be a source of fulfillment. They are meant to provide security, govern group behavior, and aid in a minimal level of physical and mental well-being of individuals in a society. Setting personal standards on the level of governmental law is like accepting the threshold of a pass-fail exam as success. Excellence isn't the goal, and knowledge gained and ability to apply it are minimally obtained and often misguided.

Many years ago, I became certified to scuba dive by completing a series of tests. I remember the final written exam. I answered all but one question correctly. The instructor praised my accomplishment as most didn't come close to answering so many correctly. Certification could be achieved by correctly answering 70 percent of the questions. I, however, was keenly interested in the one question I incorrectly answered. When it came to scuba diving, I didn't want to risk any level of incompetence. That one error could be very important. I had a strong desire for excellence. After all, it was my life on the line.

Christians are instructed to submit to governing authorities, as mentioned in many places in the Bible, including Romans 13. However, we are also taught throughout the New Testament to follow Jesus as the perfect example of excellence. We use his teaching and example to guide our personal development of discipleship.

Limiting your desire and defining your purpose by what is allowed by societal law will not allow you to define your personal principles. The standards of Christian principles are higher because they represent the character of a higher power, one that is eternal, unchanging, all-powerful, complete, and perfect in character and action and the source of truth, justice, mercy, and love. It is the difference between living a decent life and experiencing excellence. The path toward excellence is the only way to a true sense of purpose, empowerment, freedom, and fulfillment.

❧ A CASE STUDY ON DEFINING PRINCIPLES

It is against the law of most, if not all, societies to steal something that is not yours. Most people, regardless of source of principles, will never rob a bank or someone's house. Theft would be a clear violation of both societal law and Christian belief. But life can present situations that may not be so clearly defined.

For example, here is a true story that provided a heated discussion among a group of high schoolers. One of the youths bought a car from a neighbor, an older couple in need of money who had reached the age of only one driver in the house. The car needed some work to be drivable. The youth was willing to accept it as-is, where-is. Cleaning the vehicle for the first time revealed a box pushed out of sight in the far corner of the trunk. Approximately fifty silver dollars were found in the box.

The youth was presented with several different alternatives. Do you keep the box, as accepting the vehicle as-is means possession of all items within the vehicle? Or do you give it to the neighbors thinking they had not meant to leave such a treasure in the vehicle?

While thinking about this decision, ask yourself how your thoughts follow the law of the land, the influence of others, and your thoughts of Christian belief. As you think, ask yourself how important it is that the people in this account were elderly or your neighbor. What if your neighbor were unfriendly? What if the car were purchased from a third party?

Would you think differently if you found a single silver dollar rather than fifty? What if instead you found a thousand silver dollars? Even in a small group of youth, there was a multitude of strongly opinionated views of "the right thing to do."

What the youth did isn't important. Honestly, I don't remember asking what decision was made. The big question is "What would you do?" The bigger question is "Why?"

YOUR THOUGHTS?

- There are many books, blogs, and discussions otherwise that are centered on the ideas of living a principled life. Define principles as 'accepted, tried and true, rules you live by'. Write down three that come to mind that you have determined to be important to guide your decisions and actions. They can relate to work, personal relationships, or any part of your life. Consider what you might emphasize to your child, present or future. If you are having difficulty, are there principles that your parents, valued mentor, or teacher has emphasized to you?
- Do all people have principles?
- Are principles what you think, what you do, or both?
- Do different circumstances force a need for different principles, for instance, work, different social groups, age, stress, hunger, or conflict?
- Why might the display of one's principles change over time?
- Are there certain convictions, beliefs that are so absolute that you take a stand for regardless of circumstance, that others would identify you to have?
- Where do people get their foundational beliefs that are essential for a purposeful, fulfilled life?
- How can you tell that someone is a follower of Jesus?
- Read the following Biblical passages: Mark 12:28-31, Luke 16:10-12, Matthew 25:34-45, Matthew 5:43-45, Matthew 7:1-5, Matthew 23:27-28, and Matthew 6:14-15. Pick one that especially resonates with your beliefs. How does the passage relate to your principles? How does it relate to your interaction with others?

🌱 2
ME, VALUABLE? QUESTIONING YOUR WORTH

❧ A REMEMBRANCE OF CHILDHOOD

A brief eulogy in the newspaper: "Gerald ... member of the VFW, wife deceased, survived by children in various places in the U.S., service pending." As best I remember, it wasn't much to read about.

There weren't many accounts of accomplishments to let the world know the impact of his life: no civic club offices, no businesses made, or no trophies or awards mentioned. You'd think it was just an end to a more or less valueless life. I, a high school senior about to leave town for college, knew better.

I'd known him one summer of my early childhood. He was the old man who sat on the bench outside of the corner store. It seems like he was there every time I had enough money to bike down for a drink. I'd sit on the curb next to my bicycle until I finished my drink so I could return the bottle to the rack. We didn't say much to one another at first. But after an encounter or two, he would start up the conversation with something about my bike or some other childhood importance.

As the summer went on, I'd look ahead to make sure he was on the bench before I rode all the way to the store. My anticipation to visit with him almost overtook the desire for the taste of the soft drink. I didn't know it at the time, but reflection shows me just how much I valued seeing him. And I learned from him, mind you, nothing academic or technical or what one would think as career-building.

There wasn't mention of race, religion, politics, or who or what was more important than someone or something else. We just talked about stuff in a way that made me feel valuable and happy to be alive. It's hard to explain, just important stuff to a kid.

Looking back, maybe he didn't accomplish much in the world's view. He was just another old man who spent a lot of his time on a bench watching the world go by. But to me, he was a friend. I remember laughing at his jokes, listening to his stories of life, and being encouraged. You know what I mean, just the kind of stuff a kid needed.

Somehow that short-term relationship made me feel valued. And you know, even though I'm the age that others see me as that remembrance of the man more than the youth, I find I still need to feel I am valuable and life is worthwhile. Moreover, I place importance on helping others to feel the value and worthiness of life.

❧ PERSONAL VALUE

We all experience ups and downs of life: sometimes feeling very good, other times feeling very bad, and most of the time feeling somewhere in-between. Your thoughts and feelings about yourself affect every aspect of your life, especially your desire and ability to relate with others.

When you sense the ups, you are likely to see more value in your purpose for living. When you sense the downs, you may see little value in living.

Fill in the following: I feel best about myself when I _____.

Maybe you stated phrases related to accomplishments: I feel best about myself when I complete a challenge. Perhaps it is more people-related: I feel best when I'm helping others. Or it could be the following: I feel best when people tell me I'm great. (Come on! Who doesn't like that one?)

Words like *ego* and *self-esteem* can be viewed positively or negatively. We tend to gain confidence when we believe we are valuable or worthy. This confidence can increase our desire and ability to act upon our beliefs, which can be good for us and those around us. Conversely, a high sense of personal importance or worthiness may inflate egos, lessen regard for others, and lead to loneliness and isolation.

Does a low sense of self-worth allow us to be humble and more aware of the value of others? Or does it encourage inaction, isolation, and depression? The down times may ultimately benefit by leading us to refocus on living with a purpose founded on truth. However, these are also the times we may fall deeply into depression, become consumed with fear, and develop an overwhelming sense of insignificance.

Hopefully, you agree that everyone has a desire to have a high sense of personal worth and that living a purposeful life reinforces this sense. A directed, fulfilling life requires us to believe in something, more correctly someone, with great power and abilities. We can look inwardly or outwardly for that power. When we look inwardly, we see ourselves as the source of power to define and accomplish our desires.

When we look outwardly for the source of power, we rely on entities of greater power and perfection than our own abilities. Worldly examples of such include mentors, teachers, parents, and peers. Christians look upward to Jesus.

⮞ CHRISTIAN'S SENSE OF SELF-WORTH

The belief of worthiness and confidence in oneself can be very conflicting for Christians. Many years ago, a minister, Norman Vincent Peale, became known for writings that encouraged the habit of positive thoughts to succeed in relationships and careers. By his position, a strong sense of self-worth and positive outlook brings one closer to God. In turn, the result is more service to God and a positive impact on people.

Other Christian leaders countered that a strong sense of personal value would separate one from God by building up barriers of pride and egotism. Their thought was the power of positive thinking would enforce self-reliance apart from God. One then would tend to separate from the belief in the need for faith in God. The individual becomes the authority in their relationship with God. While actions may be called good because of positive personal and societal effects, they would not be sourced by God. Barriers of egotism and selfishness would impede a relationship with God.

Good works are actions that are sourced by the power of God (John 10:32). They are intended to accomplish his purpose (Romans 8:28). When sourced by faith in God, good works produce fruit of the spirit. The fruit is described in Galatians 5 as love, joy, peace, forbearance, kindness, goodness, faithfulness, gentleness, and self-control. Ephesians 2 and Philippians 2 are two additional chapters of the Bible that can help clarify God's desires for us to be conduits of his good work. The fruit of the spirit becomes more a part of what we are as we grow in our efforts to be part of God's work.

What are your thoughts on having a high sense of personal worth? Does it promote pride, judgment, and disunity? If so, that can't be good. God opposes the proud, warns of judging others, and stresses the good in unity.

> He mocks proud mockers but shows favor to the humble and oppressed. (Proverbs 3:34)

> Do not judge, or you too will be judged. For in the same way you judge others, you will be judged, and with the measure you use, it will be measured to you. (Matthew 7:1–2)

> How good and pleasant it is when God's people live together in unity! (Psalm 133:1)

Conversely, does a low sense of self-worth promote depression, weakness, and timidity? If so, that can't be desirable. God encourages his people to be joyous, strong, and courageous.

> But the fruit of the Spirit is love, joy, peace, forbearance, kindness, goodness, faithfulness, gentleness and self-control.

Against such things there is no law. (Galatians 5:22-23)

For the Spirit God gave us does not make us timid, but gives us power, love and self-discipline. (2 Timothy 1:7)

Have I not commanded you? Be strong and courageous. Do not be afraid; do not be discouraged, for the Lord your God will be with you wherever you go. (Joshua 1:9)

❧ WORTH FOUNDED UPON TWO NATURES

Establishing and focusing on the source of your worthiness will help lessen the confusion of self-worth. Our sense of worth arises from two natures: one powered by a relationship with the sinless, perfect, all-knowing, all-powerful God and the other by our nature to be in control of ourselves apart from God.

When we rely on an imperfect source, we suffer the consequences of a confused, misguided, and unfulfilled existence. And even the most narcissistic among us must admit to the imperfection and limits to self-empowerment.

You may argue that any effort toward good works regardless of source is better than none. That may be correct: When in doubt, just do good. There is plenty of opportunity to simply "get busy and do some good." You may also find obeying God's commands has positive effects on your spiritual growth regardless of motive. God understands that we are not perfect in our intentions or actions. He can use imperfection for his good works.

Fulfillment of a purpose-driven life requires actions to be sourced by God. If not, good works fall short of producing fruit of the spirit. Experiencing the fruit of the spirit reinforces our confidence and growth in the knowledge that a real sense of worth comes from God. The journey isn't easy. God provides us the power of discernment and action. Yet, no matter how intently we seek the will of God, we will still have difficulty determining and applying it to specific situations. A healthy prayer life and the disciplined reading of God's word will help us recognize God's desire and his interaction in our lives.

∽ GOD EMPOWERS

Do you believe God to be perfect, all-powerful, and loving? Do you desire a relationship with God? Do you believe that God desires to have a relationship with you? "For God so loved the world that he gave his one and only Son, that whoever believes in him shall not perish but have eternal life" (John 3:16).

Accepting God's love for us reinforces a desire to know more about him. Christians desire to grow in the knowledge and respond to the commands of God. As we grow in our dependence on God, our sense of value based on love for ourselves or recognition from anything other than God becomes less a part of our nature. That rebirth, as the Bible describes, requires a desire to please God and seek the empowerment of his Holy Spirit.

We receive a filling of the spirit as more and more room for the spirit is available within us. That requires a desire to be filled by his Holy Spirit and to remove other entities taking up the space of influence within us. On a practical basis, this may include removing ourselves from destructive influences and toward those who similarly seek God's goodness.

Restated, our desires gradually align with God as we mature in our understanding, faith, and love for God. We see God's purpose for all as our purpose for living. This path to fulfillment goes beyond self-determined effort. We gain a real sense of value and worthiness from what God accomplishes through us. Like the disciple Paul, our thoughts of personal gain as a disciple of Jesus are in opposition to those fueled by motives of self-glory (see Philippians 3).

Our relationship with God made possible by Jesus brings us confidence, courage, and strength with humbleness and a loving, caring spirit toward others. We celebrate victories with the understanding that God has given us these blessings. And faith in God's unfailing love and protection provides us courage and strength in times of struggle and failure.

We experience and respond to life differently as we grow in our knowledge and faith in God. We see opportunities in times of conflict rather than being overwhelmed by the potential for failure or pain. We don't rely as heavily on good times to make us feel valuable. Nor are we as quick to seek blame to lessen feelings of injustice and worthlessness in bad times.

With growth in our reliance on God, our sense of value isn't based on our judgment of our perceived rank among others. We can then value others without feeling that by doing so we devalue ourselves. In essence, we base our strength on our sense of worth upon God's purpose and love realizing his ways are perfect (Psalm 18:30), and his love never fails (Psalm 136:23).

✎ FAITH'S ESSENTIALNESS

Followers of Christ accept that even the best-aligned works will be imperfect and incomplete. We are imperfect and limited in our understanding of God. However, by faith and grace, we can grow in knowledge and wisdom of God's desires for us. Faith, described biblically as believing in what we can't see or understand, becomes a welcomed strength in our pursuit of purpose and fulfillment.

After all, how can we have a belief in God without faith? Aside from the inability to comprehend his all-knowing, all-powerful, all-present character, we can't fathom why God would see us so valuable as to forgive us of our continual sins and rebellion against him. Thank God he doesn't have the requirement that we fully understand him or are perfect in our desire or ability. Accepting God, seeking him, and acting upon his desires are sufficient for growth.

Think about the essentialness of faith while reading the Bible. You may find Paul's letters in the New Testament, for example, Colossians and Ephesians, good places to start for encouragement and guidance. Even though written centuries ago, the writings are relatable to what we as Christians are facing today.

✎ AM I VALUABLE?

Regardless of how strong a sense of personal worth or source of that sense, we all will have times that we question if our lives have much value. Even the most devout, mature Christian will sense times of failure and futileness. Life on earth brings many blessings and hardships. Through it all, we measure our value by the level we feel loved.

Without love, we sense isolation, lack of purpose, and failure. With love, we have relationships, assurance, and encouragement. Not to go into detail, as a latter chapter is devoted to the subject of truth and love, we question our worth when we question if we are loved.

Christians have assurance of love. What better testament is there than the birth, earthly presence, death, and resurrection of Jesus? Still, even the most mature Christian needs to be reminded of the significance of the following verse, "For God so loved the world that he gave his one and only Son, that whoever believes in him shall not perish but have eternal life" (John 3:16).

In times of doubt and uncertainty, it bears remembering that God loved you so much that he allowed Jesus to bear your sins, suffer for you, and die for you, all so you can have a relationship with him for eternity. If God would do this for you, just how valuable are you? It's likely more than you can comprehend.

YOUR THOUGHTS?

- What different entities do people use as benchmarks to measure their or others' worth?
- Do you define your worth by where your abilities rank in comparison to others?
- How might competition hinder your thoughts of personal worth?
- How might competition encourage your thoughts of personal worth?
- Do you measure your worth by your accomplishments and/or positive feedback from others?
- How might relationships affect your perception of worthiness?
- Do you become less confident when you sense a low level of self-worth?
- Do you dwell on the idea of failing prior to starting a challenge?
- How does failing to accomplish a challenge affect your behavior?
- Is a sense of high level of personal worthiness, confidence, and pride the same thing?
- Do you become more selfish as your sense of worthiness increases?
- Is being confident of your abilities a positive or negative trait?
- Where do your beliefs about personal worthiness come from?
- Does the death and resurrection of Jesus relate to your feelings of worthiness?

🌱 3
ME, LEAD?

❧ UNEXPECTED BLESSINGS

After thirty years of assisting with the same annual multi-state youth competitive event, you would think the last time would get easier. But it didn't. The host site had done little preparation. Experience told me it was destined to be a chaotic mess and, although beyond my control, I was likely to be guilty by association.

Sure enough, the first scheduled activity was chaotic. Many youths lost their opportunity to participate because of poor planning of the organizers of the event. I noticed that the rest of the management committee was absent from the scene. I had a decision to make: stand up or run away. I stood up.

My reward was being the center of attention of a circle of twenty-plus irate parents. There a lot of yelling, finger-pointing, and name-calling, and I was the only face they had to direct their anger toward. Ill-equipped and knowing others were really calling the shots, I knew this was an unfair situation for me. Nonetheless, there I was.

I had a choice to run or retaliate. I did neither. I listened to it all, not backing away or volleying defensive comments. All I could do was to look at it from their perspective and not let their anger cause me to lose my intentions of helping.

After a while, I was able to speak, assuring them that I understood and would try to help. It was good for my well-being that I was able. Once again, a mini-crisis of life had passed.

About thirty minutes later, one of the loudest—and I could add purveyor—of unfair questions about my abilities and intentions came to me and apologized. He said he was amazed at my ability to stand firm, be calm, and not retaliate. He said he usually didn't act the way he did, but this was about his girl. He told me she was all he had left. He'd lost his son at a college recently in a tragic accident.

I asked him how. He shared the story. It was too familiar to me. I knew his son. He was a well-respected student obtaining a degree in the department at the university where I was employed. Many faculty and students grieved for the loss. So at an event in Louisiana, a man from Tennessee shared his loss to me, a stranger from Oklahoma. What a coincidence!

In turn, I was able to relate to him how good of a person his son was. I could tell hearing that gave him comfort. Call it coincidence, if you want. I do, but not coincidental in the way you might think. I see it as a co-incidence with God.

There is no other reason that the one person who came to me afterward was this man. There is no other reason that he would have known how important he was to my sense of value and purpose at the time. There is no way such completeness of blessing could be reached other than God's intervention.

I knew immediately that God had blessed me as much

as the father. I felt so blessed that I was able to be at that specific location at that one event at that time. That's a sense of assurance that one only receives as a gift from God.

I concluded that event wasn't such a mess after all. I can assure you even so the same ground was covered, the long drive home was much more enjoyable than the long drive to the event. The only difference was recognizing God's authority and love along the way.

ᦸ BORN TO LEAD?

Have you ever related to the following statements: "Why ask me? I don't know what to do. Why should I be the one to make the decisions anyway? After all, I didn't ask for this, and it's well beyond my job description or pay grade. Besides, I don't have the ability or resources to fix the problems anyway."

Are you a leader? "Not me," you say. Be careful before you answer. Even the most non-social among us have some level of interaction with others. Leading and being led goes hand in hand with interaction.

Let's take driving a car as an example. Maybe you are more the type to lead the convoy on the interstate, showing you have what it takes to buck the speed limit. Or perhaps you are more likely to take a latter position in the pack, allowing the leader to take the risk of encountering a patrol car. Either way, your actions influence others' actions. In a way, our path through life is a series of episodes like being part of the pack on the interstate.

You may think it requires intent and desire to influence others. While you may not consider yourself a leader, it is impossible to not influence others. "Oh, not if I don't act," you say. Not so fast with that argument.

Not responding can just as easily influence others as action. Say you are in line buying a few grocery items and notice the person in front of you overestimated the cost of items by a few dollars more than what they have. Maybe you offer to cover the deficit. Perhaps you don't. Either way, your response affects the thoughts and actions of those around you. You have influenced those around you, whether you wanted to or not.

❧ LEADERSHIP DEFINED

Societies revere people who are leaders. Think about the number of times we are directed to workshops, books, teachings, sermons, and other exchanges about leadership. Leading others stirs up curiosity in everyone and is essential for many for fulfillment. However, leadership is also hard to define. Leadership is commonly described by attributes.

Can you list five or more attributes that help define your thoughts of a leader? Does your list include items such as knowledgeable, genuine, trustworthy, consistent, patient, optimistic, or concern for others? Does your list focus on empowering followers or the leader? Are attributes related to serving others included in your list?

I challenge you to research some quotes from significant, constructive, and able leaders in business, sports, and other areas of our world. You will find as written in the Bible, leadership requires morally-based servitude.

Not so with you. Instead, whoever wants to become great among you must be your servant, (Matthew 20:26)

Kings detest wrongdoing, for a throne is established through righteousness. (Proverbs 16:12)

❧ CHRISTIAN LEADERSHIP

Search the words *leader* or *leadership* via the internet and you will find over a hundred million potential sites. It's a subject of keen interest for both those with opinions to express and those seeking direction. Leadership requires a leader, another or others to be influenced, a goal or purpose, and a method to apply influence. It starts with a belief so strong that you are compelled to act upon it. Call it passion-fueled action.

Passion, purpose, leader, and followers are words not foreign to Christians. The uniqueness of Christian leadership is that this passion is sourced from God, gifted by Jesus's sacrifice, and guided by the Holy Spirit.

Passionate leadership is founded on love and faith. Love fuels our courage to act, and faith conquers our fears. We become passionate about our purpose when we truly accept and realize God loves us. His passion for us fuels our actions. Our actions influence people we encounter and in turn people they influence.

As followers of Jesus, we look upon him and the accounts of his life on earth for direction and knowledge on how we are to influence others. The importance of this knowledge reinforces the need to continually read and meditate on scripture.

Christ's ministry on earth was purposeful. Perhaps the most-often quoted piece of scripture is John 3:16–17.

> For God so loved the world that he gave his one and only Son, that whoever believes in him shall not perish but have eternal life. For God did not send his Son into the world to condemn the world, but to save the world through him.

To accomplish this, Jesus was clear in his purpose to do the will of God. "For I have come down from heaven not to do my will but to do the will of him who sent me." (John 6:38).

This brings to light one of the most important principles of leadership: servitude. While the naïve see leadership as an opportunity for personal glory, mature leaders see position and influence to build knowledge and ability in others. And mature leaders see leadership as a way to represent something, or someone, greater than themselves.

The account of Jesus's ministry in Matthew, Mark, Luke, and John is filled with accounts of how and what Jesus accomplished while on earth. His ministry was done not just for those who lived with him at the time. It is for our sake as much or more so. For example, what insight on Jesus's purpose is given by the following scripture?

> Jesus called them together and said, "You know that the rulers of the Gentiles lord it over them, and their high officials exercise authority over them. Not so with you. Instead,

whoever wants to become great among you must be your servant, and whoever wants to be first must be your slave—just as the Son of Man did not come to be served, but to serve, and to give his life as a ransom for many." (Matthew 20:25–28)

☙ THE INFLUENCE OF THE HOLY SPIRIT

It must have been extremely difficult for the followers of Jesus to maintain their faith in accomplishing the charge of their mission after the death and resurrection of Jesus. Confusion, discouragement, abandonment, fear, and helplessness are just a few of the thoughts that come to mind. Likely, these feelings come to mind because I sense them thousands of years later.

Fortunately we aren't left to our own accord and ability. As with the apostles of Jesus's time on earth, we have been given the Holy Spirit. The Spirit advocates our relationship with God and fuels our actions and thoughts to better know and serve God.

We are each given awareness of special gifts through the Spirit. 1 Corinthians 12 and Romans 12 might be helpful to begin a study on how the Holy Spirit acts in Christian lives. The power, guidance, and gifting of the Holy Spirit drive the desire for Christian growth. And with growth, we can expect opportunities to lead others to God's purpose.

❧ COURAGE TO ASK, COURAGE TO ACT

To sum up, we are all leaders as we have influence over others. Nothing comes close to the blessing of being a conduit for God's love. It manifests as a desire to serve others. It requires a desire to act. It starts with expressing that desire to yourself and God. While you may not have full knowledge of how to best serve others, you do have Jesus's example, the Holy Spirit, and God's instruction. As biblically stated in John 16:1–33, ask and you will receive. And by his power, grief will turn to joy.

Studying scripture, praying, and relating with other Christians will help align your desires with God's purpose for your life. You will become more aware of opportunities God provides. God's will shapes your response to opportunities.

We don't have the self-empowerment to define our path. However, we do have the power and guidance of the Holy Spirit to lead us down paths that serve God's desires. It starts with admitting your inadequacy to God, asking for forgiveness of sinning against him, and professing a desire to serve him with obedience. Do you have the courage to ask God to be a leader?

YOUR THOUGHTS?

- On a scale of 1 (low desire) to 10 (high desire), what is your level of interest in leading in the following situations?

  At work
  Hobby and recreation activities
  Family matters outside of immediate family members
  Toward peer groups
  Toward those younger than you
  Toward those older than you

- How would you rate your general desire to lead others?
- Have others looked upon you as a leader in the past?
- When are you generally most likely to desire to lead others?
- Do you believe that you can avoid being an influence on others?
- Can you think of someone you have considered your mentor?
- Can you think of someone who has considered you a mentor?
- Can you provide an example of a time that your beliefs and principles had an obvious impact on another?
- What attributes would you list as positive qualities of a leader?
- How does a person's belief in and relationship with Jesus affect their definition of leadership?
- Do you believe God intends you to be a leader?
- How does Mathew 20:25-28 relate to leadership?

🌱 4
ME, FOLLOW?

⤳ THE FOURTEEN-YEAR-OLD ME

Like other kids, my mother, in exasperation, would often relay it to me in one form or another, "If your friends jumped off a cliff, would you follow them?"

Of course, she didn't really understand me. What I saw in those I chose to follow was much different than what she saw. The big difference between our points of view was our beliefs on the intentions of those I chose to follow. Where she saw recklessness, I saw courage. Where she saw disrespect, I saw individuality. Where she saw a lack of honoring the established law, I saw crusaders. I had a desire for discovery. She had years of experience that taught her that desire would lead to trouble. I wanted independence. She was afraid of losing me.

Looking back, I suppose the truth was somewhere in between our perspectives. I also think like our parents, we as parents aren't any better at dealing with these challenges. We usually chalk up these struggles to dealing with a teenager and rely on time to be the solution.

And thank God, we made it through the struggle of

deciding whom to follow as a teenager. Or have we really? Maybe like callouses on our hands, aging has only helped us hide the pain of those struggles.

Even though we age out of our teenage years, I don't think we ever grow out of the question that was so evident during those formative years. Whom do we follow?

◟❧ FOLLOWING THE LEADER

Search for material on being a leader and you will be overwhelmed with the amount of information and opinions given on the subject. But search for information on being a follower and you will find few suggestions. Most of the information about following is related to following Jesus. It's as if the thought of following is relegated to the die-hard religious, not an attribute for success in the world.

Being admired as a follower simply isn't part of our culture. One reason for the abundance of information on leading is in our desire to be self-reliant, independent, and in control. And we relate leading with these desires.

Isn't it interesting that we are not encouraged or taught how to be a good follower, realizing that much of our time is spent on exactly that? Have you ever been on a hike through the woods? I bet you followed a path more often than blazing your own trail. It's safer and more dependable to arrive at a destination, that is, if whoever marked it has the same sense of destination as you.

◦❧ THE DANGER IN FOLLOWING OURSELVES

For some reason, the thought of following our own desires brings up the image of a dog chasing its tail. A lot of energy is expended with no forward progress. Even if accomplished, all you got a hold of is what you already had.

To some degree, we all want to oversee our own life and not be led by actions or thoughts of others. Partly that desire comes from our need for control and security. Add to those needs the thought that independence and insolation provide self-control and security. And many of the advancements of society promote just that: independence and isolation. However, those behaviors may bring negative consequences.

Our desire for independence and insolation often leads to fear, egotism, and ignorance. Caution replaces courage. We become led by fear rather than faith. We are quick to become defensive when challenged with different points of view. This sense of self-importance restricts our interest in others, and the desire to learn from others.

Left unchecked, this protectionism can build into a false sense of self-importance, so much so that you may believe you have the right to expect others to allow your actions and beliefs precedence over everything and everyone else. Your goal could become to walk—or better yet to be carried—down a comfort-driven path of self-importance. The only safe interaction then is when others act to serve you.

Maybe that scenario is too extreme. Perhaps we aren't so independent and self-centered. Possibly we are tolerant of others' views and actions. True tolerance takes courage and self-awareness. Societal norm promotes an attitude of tolerance described as "You do your thing, and I'll do my thing. I will live to not interfere with your thing. And I have the right not to be affected by your thing." This leads to constricting our definition of tolerance to times when others' views and actions don't negatively affect us. This is tolerance based on selfishness, not tolerance based on knowledge and respect.

Does that sense of self-righteousness describe our societal state in the United States? Aren't laws promoted by political parties to be "for our personal protection and good of those like us"? After all, political parties rely on protectionism and the resultant fear and conflict as motives for people to become politically active. The need for societal protectionism becomes very dominant in a country of such diversity as ours.

A desire for insulation from others often leads to isolation. Isolation resulting from the desire for independence and to be unaffected by others has negative effects on lives. Isolation from other's influence will lessen our knowledge about ourselves and others. This is especially true when we interact socially primarily by passive means such as social media. Many haven't had much active person-to-person interaction with the general public. When required to do so, the skill set to listen, interpret, and respond face-to-face is limited. So too are their perspectives.

We all tend to define and limit our perspective to circumstances of the moment at hand. We seek fairness over righteousness. Unfortunately our sense of fairness is centered most often on our needs and desires, not from the perspective of needs and desires of others. And as circumstances are ever-changing, so too does our perspective.

Our skill set and confidence to deal with the routines of life decrease without the interaction of others. This combination of ignorance based on our own sense of fairness and the inexperience of interaction increases our levels of fear and insecurity. What we claim to be a strength of independence is really a dependence on doubt and fear. The solution is to follow someone of greater power who provides a way and truth.

❧ WHO TO FOLLOW?

We may think we desire to be independent, but is independence from being led even possible? Is it what we really desire? If we are truthful, isn't even the most self-reliant person interested in the thoughts, beliefs, and principles of others? Without that interest, would there be movies, books, plays, news, sports, songs, television, scheduled meal times, internet, church, clubs, government, and so forth?

We may not want to admit it, but most of our beliefs are credited to someone else rather than what we self-formulate. We absorb commentaries from social media and advice from friends and families. We are inundated by others whose job is to influence our habits, determine how we spend our time, and define what fulfillment means.

We can take little credit for developing novel concepts or independently developing talents and abilities. We are largely a product of being led by our environment, and our environment continually expands with increases in availability of technology.

What influences your desire to follow someone or something? Admiration? Envy? Some influences simply must be avoided. We learn to cope with those we don't prefer but can't avoid. Some simply should be embraced. Most require a conscious effort to realize how much of an influence they have on you.

Decisions on who or what to follow are the most important actions in your life. It shapes your relationships, health, career, and ultimately outcomes of life and death. As stated previously, Christians are followers of Jesus.

◦❧ FOLLOWERS OF JESUS

As Christians, we profess that Jesus was born, lived, died, and was resurrected to fulfill God's promise. We believe that we are allowed a relationship with God because of the forgiveness of our sin brought about by Christ's sacrifice for us. To profess that we are Christians states that we not only believe in God, Jesus, and the Holy Spirit, but that we love and obey God. We believe God is truth and has authority over all creation. Consider the following verses.

> Jesus answered, "I am the way and the truth and the life. No one comes to the Father except through me. (John 14:16)

> Jesus said to his disciples, "Whoever wants to be my disciple must deny themselves and take up their cross and follow me." (Matthew 16:24)

> Jesus replied: "'Love the Lord your God with all your heart and with all your soul and with all your mind.' (Matthew 22:37)

But when he, the Spirit of truth, comes, he will guide you into all the truth. He will not speak on his own; he will speak only what he hears, and he will tell you what is yet to come. (John 16:13)

Follow God's example, therefore, as dearly loved children and walk in the way of love, just as Christ loved us and gave himself up for us as a fragrant offering and sacrifice to God. (Ephesians 5:1–2)

But if anyone obeys his word, love for God is truly made complete in them. This is how we know we are in him: (1 John 2:5)

"You are worthy, our Lord and God, to receive glory and honor and power, for you created all things, and by your will they were created and have their being." (Revelation 4:11)

Christians are defined by whom we believe Jesus to be. His importance in our lives fuels our passion for our purpose of living. Our desire for him urges us to seek out more about him. As such, Christians will follow instructions written in scripture, received through prayer and fasting, and gained from others with similar beliefs in Jesus.

Believing Jesus to be the Son of God and your Savior is the crucial step in pursuit of living purposely and fulfilled. This belief is much greater than simply acknowledging Jesus to be a great man or prophet who lived many years ago. By grace and God's love, we are given the ability and desire to accept that Jesus is God personified. He allows our acceptance by God and enables us to relate to God. Studying Jesus's life as documented in the Bible gives us a perfect example of a purposeful life. We are given the starting point, path, and destination. The question is, "Are you willing to follow Him?"

YOUR THOUGHTS?

- How many times a day do you think others try to lead you to make a particular choice?
- Who do you seek or have sought advice for the following situations?

  Work or career

  Financial matters such as buying large purchases with long-term debt

  Family matters such as child rearing

  Vacation choices

  Spiritual matters

- How do you discern whom to be led by?
- What attributes are important for someone to have in order to lead you?
- Is a perceived lack of need to be led by others a strength or weakness?
- Does one or the other, leading or being led, require more courage and strength?
- Does a high stature among your peers reduce the need to be influenced or led by others?
- What do Matthew 16:24, John 10:27, and Ephesians 2:1-10 state about following Christ?

PART II
SOw WHAT ABOUT GOD

"No man is an island entire of itself; every man is a piece of the continent, a part of the main" is the beginning of a meditative reading by John Donne (*Meditation XVII Devotions upon Emergent Occasions*). His premise was that humans don't thrive when isolated from others. Most of us would agree.

However, some believe that being a piece of something larger isn't best. In that thought, being a piece of something larger means we accept that something else is more important, powerful, and able than us. That position would mean we are unable to live solely by our own abilities or desires. We lose independence, self-control, power, and influence. And by losing those entities, we lose our identity and our way to fulfillment.

While many may counter that relying on a greater authority is part of their character, there are times that complete reliance wouldn't be advisable. So most believers in God's existence tend to categorize and limit God's influence to certain areas or times of their life. Even mature Christians struggle with thoughts of loss of freedom and the need for self-control.

The first part of this book is intended to encourage self-examination. Part II is meant to help you gain the courage to be guided by God to receive truth, purpose, and fulfillment. A desire for purpose and fulfillment leads to many questions. What does it mean to trust in ourselves? What does it mean to trust God? How does our trust relate to how we define right from wrong? Can obedience to God really lead to personal fulfillment?

🌱 5

WHO CAN YOU TRUST?

~• THE FOUNDATION OF TRUST

Have you ever taken one of those personality tests intended to reveal how you respond to challenges and interact with others? I've used them as tools for leadership development. Individuals first identified their tendency for a particular personality type. Then with the use of teamwork exercises, they experience how different personality types approach and solve problems in groups and as individuals. When successfully done, participants leave with a greater appreciation for people, regardless of similarities or differences.

One of the biggest obstacles faced is keeping a person's focus away from weighing the value of how others approach and respond to situations. No matter what type of personality, most people initially think their profile is the standard for everyone else. I guess it is a universal trait to think our perspectives are the center of origin for ideas.

I'll admit that I also must fight the tendency to judge the actions of others based on my personality profile. And I was trained as an instructor to help participants to avoid such thoughts. Like everyone else, I continually deal with self-centeredness.

Fortunately, these personality tests have helped me to value thoughts and actions of those with different tendencies of behavior. I'm still amazed at how differently people approach and respond to a common challenge. I have grown beyond the need to judge the validity of these differences to see how valuable they really are.

They also encouraged me to do a lot of self-evaluation. Genetic tendencies, ten years of college, three degrees earned, and several years of employment as a scientist trained me to objectively reach logical conclusions. Emotion and desire for an outcome had to be squelched so not to taint the objectivity of the data. Logic, above all, was the solution of maneuvering through life.

And then came the birth of my daughter. That blew those ideas out the window. Although she has some of the same personality traits as me, I soon discovered she was also quite different. She chose a different educational path. Her degree in fine arts trained her to visually express emotions and, as she puts it, "follow her passion." To her, that is simply logical.

My daughter and I are much alike and much different at the same time. Over time, my initial frustration with our differences has become more of an admiration. By God's grace, we share many of the same values. That makes life easier. We just have different ways of expressing those values.

And those differences are very special.

~&~ TRUSTING YOUR HEART

Unchecked, our minds are capable of many diverse ideas: some good, others bad, and a few so sick that we disgust ourselves. I vaguely recall an old movie with a line that went something like this, "We rely on our heart to control what our minds can conceive."

What does it mean to be led by your heart? It is obviously something more than the metabolic function of your heart. And it is something deeper and longer-lasting than feelings and emotion.

Wonder why conditions related to the heart are termed *coronary*? The Latin derivation for the word *heart* comes from the word *core*. More than the organ, your heart can be defined as the core of belief, senses, and desires. Your heart encompasses your physical, mental, and spiritual life.

It is hard to provide a concrete definition of heart, outside of the meaning of the organ in our bodies that pumps blood. One way to think about it is that your heart is your compass that you rely on for direction. It is the part that guides your responses to your thoughts. Heart is sensed internally as conscience, intuition, and belief. It is expressed externally as passion, desire, dedication, strength, character, and conviction. These responses are conditioned by your spirit, soul, and body. You hope that the heartfelt expressions of your thoughts lead you to your intended destination.

∾ TRUSTING YOUR MIND

Relying on your mind seems like an easy and admirable concept. We give our brain the ultimate respect as the most powerful and complex organ. Hence, we use the phrase "It's not brain surgery" rather than "It's not liver surgery." Your brain is in control of all the functions of your body. It is so in control that it doesn't require consciousness to stay alive. Your subconscious takes care of vital bodily functions. You don't have to think about the essentials like breathing, pumping blood, or removing toxic substances from your body.

It's a little weird, but think of your brain as an independent entity designed to function for its own survival. We give our brains a lot of slack, so much so that when we do something so offensive that no other excuse would defend, we say, "I don't know. I must not have been thinking" or "I must have been out of my mind." We are quick to offer up excuses to offset the responsibility to think.

∾ TRUSTING MORE THAN HEART AND MIND

Age, experience, and help from God have shown that simply relying on what can be understood or felt isn't enough for living with purpose and fulfillment. Even so, we spend a lot of energy trying to reach those goals by our own abilities.

We try to gain power and influence over our peers. We try to gain social status by increasing our position of wealth. We try to work hard. We try devotion to family, service in good causes, and hobbies that pique our interests and challenge our abilities. These pursuits can provide positive outcomes for others and ourselves. However, there is most often a sense that the value of these pursuits is incomplete and short-lived. There is something—or more accurately someone—missing in these attempts.

As scripture notes that we were made in the image of God, we likely are given a sense that our purpose and source of fulfillment comes from God even before accepting Jesus as our Savior. When we trust Jesus to be whom he says he is, we more clearly understand the path to God, the real source of truth, purpose, and fulfillment. And it is all based on faith.

This journey of faith in God isn't an easy path. Scripture describes faith as confidence in what we hope for and assurance about what we do not see (Hebrews 11:1). Human nature leads us to doubt anything beyond the tangible, that is, what can be precisely defined and physically sensed. As we have all been let down by substitutes of faith, experience suggests we remain cautious of placing our faith entirely on anything or anyone.

Jesus gives us help and guidance along the way from the Holy Spirit. But it still takes a lot of courage to give up so much self-control. Faith isn't something we can manufacture by our own efforts. But we can receive it from Jesus, the pioneer and perfecter of faith (Hebrews 12:2). It comes from hearing the message of Jesus, which comes from the word about him. "Consequently, faith comes from hearing the message, and the message is heard through the word about Christ" (Romans 10:17).

The book of Colossians may be helpful reading for encouragement to trust Christ. For example, consider the following instruction. "Since, then, you have been raised with Christ, set your hearts on things above, where Christ is, seated at the right hand of God. Set your minds on things above, not on earthly things" (Colossians 3:1–2).

This instruction given two thousand years ago specifically instructs us to set both our heart and mind on things above. When attempting to do so, we sometimes sense that our hearts and minds are working together. Other times it seems our heart is leading us one way and our mind another.

✎ HEART FOR GOD

Previously heart was explained as the core of our senses and desires. There are many biblical examples of individuals who had a "heart for God." Possibly most often, David is thought of as a person who had a heart for God. His anointing and resulting action to confront Goliath showed his belief in the power of God as a young man (See 1 Samuel 16–17). His life chronicled in 1 and 2 Samuel was a testament to his heart for God. The book of Psalm is filled with examples of his self-expressed desire to have a heart for God.

Make no mistake. David fell to the temptation of rebellion from God. You will find ample evidence of it in your study of his actions. Having a heart for God doesn't mean you are perfect in your service to God, actions toward others, or in complete control of selfishness. His heart for God allowed David's forgiveness and alignment to follow God.

How important is a heart for God? "Blessed are the pure in heart, for they will see God" (Matthew 5:8).

This and other instructions given by Jesus emphasized

the need for God to be at the core of our essence (Read Matthew 6 and 19). There is also futility in trying to hide what is in our hearts. Jesus's words in Luke 6:43–45 bears this out.

> No good tree bears bad fruit, nor does a bad tree bear good fruit. Each tree is recognized by its own fruit. People do not pick figs from thornbushes, or grapes from briers. A good man brings good things out of the good stored up in his heart, and an evil man brings evil things out of the evil stored up in his heart. For the mouth speaks what the heart is full of.

❧ VALUING GOOD THOUGHTS

Can you live simply by what you think? How do you know if your brain is telling you the truth? What if your brain has received or is sending wrong information? What if your brain craves sensation over the survival of the body? Isn't this what we call addiction?

Let's look at instruction from the Bible as to what we should be thinking about.

> Finally, brothers and sisters, whatever is true, whatever is noble, whatever is right, whatever is pure, whatever is lovely, whatever is admirable—if anything is excellent or praiseworthy—think about such things. (Philippians 4:8)

Most everyone, regardless of Christian or not, will agree that these are desirable attributes we like to see in ourselves and others. How you define and express these traits depend on your understanding of the source of your beliefs. What actions come to mind when you hear the words in Philippians 4:8?

Are thoughts really that important? Haven't you been instructed sometime in your life that it doesn't hurt to look as long as you don't touch? Jesus taught differently.

> You have heard that it was said, "You shall not commit adultery." But I tell you that anyone who looks at a woman lustfully has already committed adultery with her in his heart. (Matthew 5:27–28)

Thoughts may seem to be unimportant to us because unlike actions, we can pretend that our thoughts don't exist or affect others. So why are thoughts so important to Jesus? Maybe Jesus wants us to realize that our thoughts are the initial stages of our actions. More importantly, perhaps it is how our thoughts affect us personally. Impure thoughts, thoughts of deception, and selfish motives build barriers to our relationship with God.

To be safe, is the best advice than to simply "not think too much"? If so, how do we explain why Jesus continuously challenged those who listened to him to think, especially by the use of parables? Parables challenge us to change our way of thinking and to develop a relationship-based outlook on issues.

Parables also promote a sense of personal discovery of the story's message. The sense of personal discovery personalizes our relationship with God. His truth is intended to be a part of who we are rather than simply what we consider to be important tools to live a good life.

↝ GOOD THOUGHTS AREN'T ENOUGH

Ever play the game of hide-and-seek? Were you the type to want to hide more than seek? Most people get a lot of pleasure from finding a good hiding place.

It's easy enough to hide in our thoughts. We've developed more than enough technology to separate us from others 24-7. But are good thoughts or best intentions enough for fulfillment? Or do we need to place our thoughts into action?

Several years ago, we were shopping in a crowded mall. Suddenly, a single cry, "MAMA!", could be heard over the noise of the crowd. I looked down the balcony to see a young child standing in the middle of the walkway yelling for her mother, who was obviously not where she needed to be. In an instant, my mind was flooded with thoughts, *Someone needs to help her. What kind of mother would let that happen? I would do something if I were closer.*

Meanwhile, a teenage girl walking alongside a friend stopped and ran back to the little girl. The teenager dropped to her knees and talked to the girl while looking around with an expression of "What am I supposed to do to help the little girl?" All the while, she was providing what was needed, consoling and assuring the child. No one else responded. Fortunately, the missing mom quickly arrived at the scene.

My inaction negatively affected the little girl and me. The teenager's action affected both positively. Why didn't we all stop what we were doing and respond even though unsure of what needed done? At the least, why didn't I go up to the teenager afterward and tell her how her actions encouraged me?

Her actions reminded me of how we become conditioned with age to not respond as God intends. We let our excuses overcome our enthusiasm and faith in God. We know better. We have been taught better.

> On one occasion an expert in the law stood up to test Jesus. "Teacher," he asked, "what must I do to inherit eternal life?" "What is written in the Law?" he replied. "How do you read it?" He answered, "'Love the Lord your God with all your heart and with all your soul and with all your strength and with all your mind; and, Love your neighbor as yourself." "You have answered correctly," Jesus replied. "Do this and you will live." But he wanted to justify himself, so he asked Jesus, "And who is my neighbor?"

> In reply Jesus said: "A man was going down from Jerusalem to Jericho, when he was attacked by robbers. They stripped him of his clothes, beat him and went away, leaving him half dead. A priest happened to be going down the same road, and when he saw the man, he passed by on the other side. So too, a Levite, when he came to the place and saw him, passed by on the other side. But a Samaritan, as he traveled, came where the man was; and when he saw him, he took pity on him. He went to him and bandaged his wounds,

pouring on oil and wine. Then he put the man on his own donkey, brought him to an inn and took care of him. The next day he took out two denarii and gave them to the innkeeper. 'Look after him,' he said, 'and when I return, I will reimburse you for any extra expense you may have.' Which of these three do you think was a neighbor to the man who fell into the hands of robbers? The expert in the law replied, "The one who had mercy on him." Jesus told him, "Go and do likewise." (Luke 10:25–37)

My excuses to not respond could fill pages of text. To be honest, it usually comes down to my preference for inaction over action. The reason I prefer inaction is that action requires interaction, which may have messy, uncontrolled outcomes. Moreover, I have fear of being wrong or more so being wronged.

We must ask ourselves the question: What is right, and do I have the courage to act upon it?

~ GOD'S GUIDANCE

Look again at Colossians 3:1–2. "Since, then, you have been raised with Christ, set your hearts on things above, where Christ is, seated at the right hand of God. Set your minds on things above, not on earthly things."

Notice the word *set*. Being instructed to set your heart and mind suggests that with God's help, we share in the ability, moreover the responsibility, to direct our hearts and minds consciously, continuously, and consistently toward God. Scripture refers to this ability as our free will.

Our interest in "Setting our hearts and minds on things above" depends on the level of importance we place on God in our life. It also depends on the confidence we have in trusting God. It requires us to know and by faith follow God's instruction. This isn't some half-full, halfway action.

> We demolish arguments and every pretension that sets itself up against the knowledge of God, and we take captive every thought to make it obedient to Christ. (2 Corinthians 10:5)

Notice in 2 Corinthians 10:5 we are instructed to demolish argument and every pretension. Does it say compromise, dwell on, tolerate, or live with it? Those words are not the same as demolish. What comes to mind when you hear the word *demolish*? I picture a demolition crew tearing down and removing a building.

Also what are pretensions? Funny, when you break down the word, you read it as pre-TENSION. Tension is felt because we set ourselves up to make excuses to disobey God, pretend God isn't whom he says he is, and pull away from his truth.

The second part of 2 Corinthians 10:5 instructs us to "take captive every thought to make it obedient to Christ." "Take captive" tells us that we are empowered and entrusted by God. Using an analogy of a boat, we are to set a true course and steer toward the destination, regardless of adversity and hardship. Simply put, we should stay true to our purpose in life.

❧ THE QUEST FOR FULFILLMENT

Even the most cynical among us desire a purposeful life. Without it, we lack fulfillment. But desiring to have purpose isn't enough. As Proverbs 3:5–6 teaches, our success to stay on course requires reliance on God. "Trust in the LORD with all your heart and lean not on your own understanding; in all your ways submit to him, and he will make your paths straight."

Trust with all your heart and submit in all your ways makes sense, doesn't it? How can one be filled completely if trusting with half a heart and submitting halfway? Wouldn't that mean that you believe you have purpose but are willing to let your path be halfway straight or be satisfied with reaching the desired destination halfway? Any wonder why feelings of futileness, worthlessness, loneliness, and fear are so evident in our lives? Fulfillment requires all-out, on course, desire to trust by faith.

Our ability to be on course requires knowledge of God's righteousness. "There is a way that appears to be right, but in the end it leads to death. The simple believe anything, but the prudent give thought to their steps" (Proverbs 14:12,15).

How futile and disappointing it would be to set a course and hold to it but end in the wrong destination because we didn't trust God, didn't ask for directions, or simply chose to remain ignorant.

So what can we do to become smarter, more passionate, and more able to move toward a purposeful and fulfilled life? Here is some additional instruction in scripture.

> Put to death, therefore, whatever belongs
> to your earthly nature: sexual immorality,

impurity, lust, evil desires and greed, which is idolatry. Because of these, the wrath of God is coming. You used to walk in these ways, in the life you once lived. But now you must also rid yourselves of all such things as these: anger, rage, malice, slander, and filthy language from your lips. Do not lie to each other, since you have taken off your old self with its practices and have put on the new self, which is being renewed in knowledge in the image of its Creator. (Colossians 3:5–10)

Therefore, as God's chosen people, holy and dearly loved, clothe yourselves with compassion, kindness, humility, gentleness and patience. Bear with each other and forgive one another if any of you has a grievance against someone. Forgive as the Lord forgave you. And over all these virtues put on love, which binds them all together in perfect unity. Let the peace of Christ rule in your hearts, since as members of one body you were called to peace. And be thankful. Let the message of Christ dwell among you richly as you teach and admonish one another with all wisdom through psalms, hymns, and songs from the Spirit, singing to God with gratitude in your hearts. And whatever you do, whether in word or deed, do it all in the name of the Lord Jesus, giving thanks to God the Father through him. (Colossians 3:12–17)

We are clearly instructed to control our thoughts and steer away from certain actions that lead to wrong destinations. However, moving toward something requires more than simply moving away from something else. We truly begin to know what fulfillment and purpose are when the desire to move toward God becomes as primal to our sense of survival as hunger and thirst. "Blessed are those who hunger and thirst for righteousness, for they will be filled" (Matthew 5:6).

And it is by Jesus that we have been brought to fullness. "For in Christ all the fullness of the Deity lives in bodily form, and in Christ you have been brought to fullness. He is the head over every power and authority" (Colossians 2:9–10).

How futile our efforts are to pursue fullness by any means.

YOUR THOUGHTS?

- Do any of the following describe you: logical, planner, impulsive, scatterbrained, emotional, unemotional, reactive, social, loner, quick-tempered, mild, quiet, shy, or bold?
- Can you think of other words that better describe yourself?
- Do you tend to socialize with others with similar personalities as yourself? Or are you drawn to those that differ?
- Has your personality changed with age?
- Do circumstances alter your personality?
- Are there certain areas of your life that you rely more on your heart than your mind or vice versa? What about relationships? What about career decisions?
- What or whom do you look toward for guidance on purpose and fulfillment?
- Can you define your goal for your purpose for living?
- Does your belief in God influence your goal for your purpose of living?
- Describe how faith and trust affect Christian relationship with God.
- If you believe that Jesus is your authority, can you say you are actively growing in your obedience to him?

🌱 6
IS THAT RIGHT?

❧ OLD WEST MOVIE JUSTICE

I enjoy many of the old Western movies. I have from early days of youth. I know they have many faults: violence, gun worship, prejudice, and stereotyping of gender and people groups. (I suppose I could argue that identifying those injustices at an early age helped me define my stance of opposition to them.) It wasn't the faults I enjoyed. Like the themes of many modern-day science fiction and superhero movies, it was the simple lesson most taught.

It was the white-hat heroes versus the black-hat bad guys. Most had a simple life lesson: Right and wrong have consequences, and it is better for everyone to do right. These movies were usually in a setting where governmental law was absent or, at the most, ineffective. Survival meant people had to be largely responsible for their own safety and protection. Danger, evil men, hunger, thirst, death, and disease were prevalent. Even so, individuals had a sense of freedom to choose right or wrong. And the consequences of actions, right or wrong, were usually sudden and irreversible.

There are not as many Western movies nowadays. Maybe the world doesn't want to be reminded of the good versus bad theme of the old Westerns unless it is in a galaxy far, far away. I wish that weren't so. To be honest, the anticipation of action, wild horses, and open spaces are also part of my fondness for Western movies. But I like to think there is much more to it. They made me think about the concept of right and wrong and who or what I was going to allow defining it for me.

⤳ RIGHT FROM WRONG

"That's not right!" We have heard it and said it what seems a million times. What is your definition of right and wrong? How do you determine right from wrong? We prefer siding with what we believe to be right based on our perception of truth, justice, and mercy. It all starts with what or with whom you base your definition of fairness and justice upon.

We all accept some standard of right and wrong is necessary. Societies rely upon the legality of a particular situation or action. However, even legality has opinion at its root. Judicial opinions can and often do differ between courts. The Supreme Court has multiple judges so a single opinion doesn't drive decision-making. Placing standards of right and wrong based on circumstances, group opinion, or solely upon the law of the land leads to unstable positions and beliefs.

Hopefully, we spend most of our time outside of the court system so we don't rely on societal legality to determine right from wrong. Maybe we determine it independently by what feels right at the time. We may defer to others or stand with the prevailing thought of the majority. Relying on these methods leads our belief into relativism, meaning there is no absolute truth and that morality varies with individual thought. This in turn promotes passivity and a personal sense of instability.

Hopefully, the law of the land originates from a source of truth, justice, and mercy. Laws in the United States are largely biblically based. For example, laws described in Leviticus may seem archaic with little bearing for today's society. Read and you will find among other relatable topics the basis for our property laws and illegality of theft, murder, and marriage of closely related family members. The point is that the position of right versus wrong requires a standard. Christians see Jesus as the standard of righteousness.

❧ CHRISTIAN BELIEF OF RIGHT AND WRONG

Christians believe in God, Jesus, and the Holy Spirit. We believe truth, justice, and mercy come from God. We believe God is absolutely and perfectly right all the time without compromise. His attributes, character, and position are the basis of right. We don't fully understand God's actions, and to be honest, we even question them. Nonetheless, by faith, we rely upon his guidance for defining right from wrong.

Our beliefs and actions are justified (positioned) to be right when we are aligned with God's character. When so, we gain an understanding of God's authority. We are provided the power of faith to persevere when we are unsure of his desire and purpose. We rely upon his grace and mercy when we mess up. And we are aware that our actions are a testament to others.

Do you think that God's definition of what is right or wrong changes? The following scripture highlights the unchanging nature of God as it relates to right versus wrong.

> The LORD within her is righteous; he does no wrong. Morning by morning he dispenses his justice, and every new day he does not fail, yet the unrighteous know no shame. (Zephaniah 3:5)

> People swear by someone greater than themselves, and the oath confirms what is said and puts an end to all argument. Because God wanted to make the unchanging nature of his purpose very clear to the heirs of what was promised, he confirmed it with an oath. God did this so that, by two unchangeable things in which it is impossible for God to lie, we who have fled to take hold of the hope set before us may be greatly encouraged. We have this hope as an anchor for the soul, firm and secure. It enters the inner sanctuary behind the curtain, where our forerunner, Jesus, has entered on our behalf. (Hebrews 6:16-20)

> As for God, his way is perfect: The LORD's word is flawless; he shields all who take refuge in him. (2 Samuel 22:31)

Atheists and agnostics do not have the belief in God that allows them to accept God's authority. Without this belief, what entities are relied upon for guidance on right and wrong? Is it possible to believe nothing is eternal? Are standards nonexistent? Is the definition of justice limited to the time at hand? Does circumstance dictate direction? People groups have wrestled with nonbelief in God and his righteousness since creation.

> Gather together and come; assemble, you fugitives from the nations. Ignorant are those who carry about idols of wood, who pray to gods that cannot save. Declare what is to be, present it—let them take counsel together. Who foretold this long ago, who declared it from the distant past? Was it not I, the Lord? And there is no God apart from me, a righteous God and a Savior; there is none but me. (Isaiah 45:20–21)

❧ A RIGHTEOUS GOD

As Christians, we believe God is righteous. He is just, and his laws are above all else. Our belief of right and wrong is sourced from his nature. The more we seek God and do what he desires, the more we understand and desire righteousness. But we are not perfect. We mess up, no matter how hard we try to be positioned rightfully. We don't meet God's standards of perfection or his state of righteousness. We think and do things that are contrary to God's character.

These thoughts and actions are separate from God's

character, and they are not acceptable to him. We call it sin. God doesn't accept sin. He couldn't any more sin than separate himself from himself. He detests sin. Consider the following verses from Scripture.

> But your iniquities have separated you from your God; your sins have hidden his face from you, so that he will not hear. (Isaiah 59:2)

> He is the Rock, his works are perfect, and all his ways are just. A faithful God who does no wrong, upright and just is he. (Deuteronomy 32:4)

> for all have sinned and fall short of the glory of God (Romans 3:23)

So does that mean if we aren't perfect, we are to be separated from God? After all, we all fall short of being perfect and without sin. If we think we are perfect, our definition of sin isn't complete and absolute. Left to our own ability, our sin creates a barrier to God's acceptance of us. Can we gain his acceptance by doing more good deeds than bad, keeping a self-defined contract so to speak? We need something beyond ourselves and abilities; we need a covenant. Christ's presence and actions provide that covenant.

❧ THE GIFT OF A COVENANT

Covenant is a word uncommon outside religious circles. Covenants are not something we routinely come upon in our daily routines and relationships. We live by contractual relationships more so than covenanted relationships. Contracts are conditional and met by completing a transfer of something we own such as property.

It is assumed that we will meet the conditions of a contract through our efforts, and when we do, we complete the contract. If we fail, we break the conditions of the contract and lose all rights to what we are to receive. These conditions would be lawful and just under the conditions of a contract.

Take the example of ordering food at a drive-thru food place. You verbally place an order for food. The business employee agrees to provide what you ordered. You agree to provide the required money. You don't pay; you don't get the food. They mess up the order; they make it right or refund your money. That's a contract.

Thankfully, we are given a covenant with God rather than a contract. Otherwise, having a relationship with a Holy God would be impossible. He is sinless. We sin. Our best intentions, efforts, and offerings have shortcomings. On our own, we haven't anything to exchange for his acceptance to fulfill a contract of relationship.

We are incapable to make or fulfill contracts with God. If heaven were a fast-food place, we wouldn't even be allowed to get in the line to order. Wow, banished from the fast-food lane of living a fulfilled life because of contract failure. I don't remember a biblical parable using fast food, but several stress the futility of self-justification versus the covenant of salvation provided by Christ.

Covenants are relationship-based rather than performance-based. The words *covering* and *covenant* are related. We are provided the blessings of the relationship by an act of someone who covers and forgives our shortcomings. As Christians, we believe that Jesus provides us a covenant with God.

We believe in Jesus as Christ to be our Lord and Savior and to be the Son of God. By his sacrificial death and resurrection on our behalf, Jesus took on our sins and paid the price for our failings and imperfections. This covenant is completely under God's authority, and it is given to us from his love, grace, and mercy. We don't earn it. We are worthy of the relationship only because God has deemed us worthy.

By Jesus, we can confess and ask God to forgive us of our sins. We are forgiven by him. We seek God and strive to live by his instruction and example. To help, we are provided the guidance and power of the Holy Spirit.

This covenant brings us blessings of love, purpose, protection, truth, justice, and mercy. We are given faith to believe in what we don't understand. We are excluded from a temporary existence and eternal death. In fact, we are given eternal life and communion with him. And we are empowered to demonstrate God's love so others can accept his existence and forgiveness.

⮞ RIGHTEOUSNESS OF GOD

God is righteous. We are provided insight on righteousness by reference of God's character in the Bible. That insight gives us knowledge of what he wants us to be and to show others. What characteristics of God are evidenced by the following verses? How do they relate to how we are to behave and relate with others?

Jesus Christ is the same yesterday and today and forever. (Hebrews 13:8)

Every good and perfect gift is from above, coming down from the Father of the heavenly lights, who does not change like shifting shadows. (James 1:17)

For his anger lasts only a moment, but his favor lasts a lifetime; weeping may stay for the night, but rejoicing comes in the morning. (Psalm 30:5)

Praise the LORD, my soul, and forget not all his benefits—who forgives all your sins and heals all your diseases, who redeems your life from the pit and crowns you with love and compassion, (Psalm 103:2–4)

Whoever does not love does not know God, because God is love. (1 John 4:8)

The Lord is not slow in keeping his promise, as some understand slowness. Instead he is patient with you, not wanting anyone to perish, but everyone to come to repentance. (2 Peter 3:9)

And the peace of God, which transcends all understanding, will guard your hearts and your minds in Christ Jesus. (Philippians 4:7)

Do you not know? Have you not heard? The Lord is the everlasting God, the Creator of the ends of the earth. He will not grow tired or weary, and his understanding no one can fathom. (Isaiah 40:28)

These are but a few Bible verses that help to understand the righteous nature of God. As a disclaimer, there is an inherent danger of listing particular verses to illustrate a point. As the entire Bible is a testament to the nature of God, the more you study scripture, the more you gain clarity of God's righteousness.

All Scripture is God-breathed and is useful for teaching, rebuking, correcting, and training in righteousness, so that the servant of God may be thoroughly equipped for every good work. (2 Timothy 3:16-17)

YOUR THOUGHTS?

- Think of all the unjust actions that have occurred through history because of differences of thought on what is right or wrong. Even those who believe in the same source of truth and righteousness are at odds with one another. Many of those who fought in the American Civil War felt that because they believed in God, somehow God was on their side. This, in essence, meant God wasn't for the opposing side.

- Do you agree that everyone must rely on a source of truth, mercy, and justice to define whether they are "in the right"?

- Where does your sense of truth, mercy, and justice come from?

- How does where we live, who we associate with, and what we are taught affect our definition of right and wrong?

- How prone are you to allow others to define your sense of right and wrong?

- How do you evaluate whether something or someone is right?

- How prone are you to act upon your sense of right and wrong?

- Should your actions be the opposite of what you believe to be right?

- How would you explain to your friends what "righteous" means to you?

- Is it likely that your friends perceive righteous behavior in a negative manner?

- Can we be right and God wrong about something?

- How do the following Biblical passages relate to the basis of right and wrong?

  2 Samuel 22:31
  Isaiah 45:20,21
  James 1.17
  Psalm 103: 2-4
  Isaiah 40:28

7
FREE TO OBEY

BURNED OUT BUT NOT BURNED UP

Do you ever feel like a rat running along the wheel in a cage? If you're honest, you must answer yes. I've been there. Even though I have been blessed to have chosen a career path that had many benefits, thirty years of doing many of the same routines, dealing with the same pressures, and not finding new solutions to old problems led to many periods of burnout.

I've seen the same in many people regardless of job, family life, wealth, or status. I suppose those even in the best careers get an occasional bout of burnout. Being the chocolate taster at a candy bar factory sounds like a good job to me, but I wonder if the person who does that even likes the taste of chocolate after a while.

I've learned to deal with feeling burned out by focusing on the freedom I receive through my obedience to God. That may sound counterintuitive, freedom sourced from obedience. But I can't say it any clearer. While disappointments were sure to come, I have felt the freedom to control my responses. That freedom has allowed me to recover from bad experiences without the experiences controlling who I am.

I have felt God's power of hope and courage at times I have felt powerless. While I have faced scary situations, I have had the love of God to feel protected. While there can be plenty of fear about the future, my faith in God gives me the freedom of security in his love for me. I may get burned out, but never will I be burned up.

~ OBEDIENCE IS UNESCAPABLE

Even the most independent and powerful person obeys something or someone. Accounts of people obeying and disobeying God are provided from beginning to end throughout the Bible. You can start with Adam and Eve in the book of Genesis and read the Bible through the warnings given to churches in Revelation. You will discover many blessings given to those who obey. You will also read of the consequences of disobedience.

We all obey something. If not God, it is most likely obedience to our selfish desires. Christians speak of this as old self and new self.

> So I tell you this, and insist on it in the Lord, that you must no longer live as the Gentiles do, in the futility of their thinking. They are darkened in their understanding and separated from the life of God because of the ignorance that is in them due to the hardening of their hearts. Having lost all sensitivity, they have given themselves over

to sensuality so as to indulge in every kind of impurity, and they are full of greed.

That, however, is not the way of life you learned when you heard about Christ and were taught in him in accordance with the truth that is in Jesus. You were taught, with regard to your former way of life, to put off your old self, which is being corrupted by its deceitful desires; to be made new in the attitude of your minds; and to put on the new self, created to be like God in true righteousness and holiness. (Ephesians 4:17–24)

Don't you know that when you offer yourselves to someone as obedient slaves, you are slaves of the one you obey—whether you are slaves to sin, which leads to death, or to obedience, which leads to righteousness? But thanks be to God that, though you used to be slaves to sin, you have come to obey from your heart the pattern of teaching that has now claimed your allegiance. You have been set free from sin and have become slaves to righteousness. (Romans 6:16–18)

There are several interesting points in the preceding scripture. Those who reject God are darkened in their understanding by the ignorance that comes with hardening of heart to God. That makes sense if you believe God to be truth.

Another way to think about it is rebellion against God's

authority leads to ignorance, impurity, and greed. Obeying God opens the path to knowledge, purity, and truth. The result is freedom from sin and the temporary sense of fulfilment it offers.

While the thought of being a slave to anything can at first seem repulsive, becoming a slave to obedience to God comes from a willingness from our heart. Our obedience is from an outflowing of our love for him. We obey because we know we are not capable to help ourselves. We desire life over the death that separation from God brings. We can think of it as accepting the invitation to fully realize God's purpose for our life.

We can have successful careers, caring friends and family, and other blessings. They are all part of us. Dedicating ourselves to God allows us to use all our parts to spread the glory of God. His purpose is our purpose, and we are filled with his Spirit as we grow toward that purpose.

Those who haven't gone through the salvation experience may think obedience to God is too restrictive and only meant to keep them from having a good time. Even those who have been saved become complacent in belief in the authority of God, compartmentalize God's authority to specific areas of their life or go through periods of rebellion. It happens to all of us to some level at one time or another. We think we will gain something of value through disobedience.

If we are honest, we can expect any sense of satisfaction gained away from God to be short-lived and short of fulfilling. The best we can ask for is what we think will be a short-term escape from God's authority. Unfortunately, escape from God is the last thing we are really wanting.

We are really wanting to escape from ourselves. That's the deception of sin.

> When you were slaves to sin, you were free from the control of righteousness. What benefit did you reap at that time from the things you are now ashamed of? Those things result in death! But now that you have been set free from sin and have become slaves of God, the benefit you reap leads to holiness, and the result is eternal life. For the wages of sin is death, but the gift of God is eternal life in Christ Jesus our Lord. (Romans 6:20–23).

~ OBEDIENCE FOUNDED ON LOVE

Those who reject or deny Jesus's lordship may do so because of the fear of giving something up. The salvation experience of "dying to the old self and being born to the new self" provides believers the power to transform their way of thinking. Paul, the author of many biblical letters of the New Testament, writes of this often, possibly most eloquently in the book of Philippians.

> But whatever were gains to me I now consider loss for the sake of Christ. What is more, I consider everything a loss because of the surpassing worth of knowing Christ Jesus my Lord, for whose sake I have lost all things. I consider them garbage, that I may gain Christ and be found in him, not

having a righteousness of my own that comes from the law, but that which is through faith in Christ—the righteousness that comes from God on the basis of faith. I want to know Christ—yes, to know the power of his resurrection and participation in his sufferings, becoming like him in his death, and so, somehow, attaining to the resurrection from the dead. (Philippians 3:7–11)

Jesus's sacrifice for our sins provides the opportunity for us to obey God through a relationship founded on the love Jesus has for us. "And this is love: that we walk in obedience to his commands. As you have heard from the beginning, his command is that you walk in love" (2 John 1:6).

Obedience to God is founded on love. Maybe that's why we have such a desire for it. Restrictive? Yes, Christians restrict behaviors and actions that lead toward destruction, sin, and spiritual death. Why? Because mature Christians love Jesus and love others. We lose the desire for actions that are against God's desire for us. It isn't as much a sense of restriction as it is a valued gift to participate in God's purpose.

Obedience requires discipline. From a worldly view, discipline can be seen as punishment to correct some undesired behavior. From a Christian view, discipline means to advance and prepare by instruction. Obedience requires strength. From a worldly view, the source of strength lies in our own abilities. From a Christian view, strength comes from God.

Obedience also requires perseverance. From a worldly view, perseverance means we are dutifully continuing to survive in times of conflict. As a Christian, we are given the gift of perseverance as an ability to continue to grow in a state of grace as we move toward a state of glory with God.

As such, the discipline of reading God's word, praying, and meeting with believers are welcomed gifts for growth. As we mature in our faith and works that come from faith, we receive God's blessing of freedom to walk with and receive power from the Spirit of God. Paul writes about this in his letter to the Galatian church.

> You, my brothers and sisters, were called to be free. But do not use your freedom to indulge the flesh; rather, serve one another humbly in love. For the entire law is fulfilled in keeping this one command: "Love your neighbor as yourself." If you bite and devour each other, watch out or you will be destroyed by each other.

> So I say, walk by the Spirit, and you will not gratify the desires of the flesh. For the flesh desires what is contrary to the Spirit, and the Spirit what is contrary to the flesh. They are in conflict with each other, so that you are not to do whatever you want. But if you are led by the Spirit, you are not under the law.

> The acts of the flesh are obvious: sexual immorality, impurity and debauchery; idolatry and witchcraft; hatred, discord, jealousy, fits of rage, selfish ambition,

dissensions, factions and envy; drunkenness, orgies, and the like. I warn you, as I did before, that those who live like this will not inherit the kingdom of God.

But the fruit of the Spirit is love, joy, peace, forbearance, kindness, goodness, faithfulness, gentleness and self-control. Against such things there is no law. Those who belong to Christ Jesus have crucified the flesh with its passions and desires. Since we live by the Spirit, let us keep in step with the Spirit. Let us not become conceited, provoking and envying each other. (Galatians 5:13–26)

✒ CHURCH

Before leaving the subject of obedience, it is worthwhile to mention the value of corporate worship and fellowship. The Christian church has the perfection of Jesus at its foundation of identity. It was commissioned by him to be part of our identity. It is the union of believers in and with Christ Jesus.

As such, participating in Jesus Christ's church is essential. It is how we collectively glorify and worship God. We receive training for discipleship and opportunities for evangelism through participating with a group of Christians in a church. Unfortunately it's natural to limit thoughts of a relationship with God to the confines of ordinances and practices of a particular church rather than as a member of Jesus Christ's church.

Jesus Christ's church cannot be defined as a building or

limited in scope by the ideology of a particular Christian group. And it is much more than what can be produced by thoughts and programs of its members. Keep in mind that although Christ's church is founded and commissioned by Jesus, the perfector of our faith, it is tended and attended by imperfect people. And we are all imperfect.

Too many people reject church participation because of these imperfections. Excuses are made on the basis of avoiding hypocrisy. Personal involvement is limited because of disagreements and suspicion of church leaders' motives. Legitimately, some churches are driven by false teaching meant to deceive people from the truth. Nothing new here. The biblical letters that follow the book of Acts address similar issues in the early church.

> But there were also false prophets among the people, just as there will be false teachers among you. They will secretly introduce destructive heresies, even denying the sovereign Lord who bought them—bringing swift destruction on themselves. Many will follow their depraved conduct and will bring the way of truth into disrepute. In their greed these teachers will exploit you with fabricated stories. Their condemnation has long been hanging over them, and their destruction has not been sleeping. (2 Peter 2:1-3)

> Dear friends, do not believe every spirit, but test the spirits to see whether they are from God, because many false prophets have gone out into the world. This is how you can recognize the Spirit of God: Every spirit that

acknowledges that Jesus Christ has come in the flesh is from God, but every spirit that does not acknowledge Jesus is not from God. This is the spirit of the antichrist, which you have heard is coming and even now is already in the world. (1 John 4:1-3).

Knowing there will be false prophets and spirits places the responsibility on Christians to mature in their understanding of God's word and character. It also emphasizes the need for membership in a particular church to be based on the core beliefs of the body of believers over facilities or programs that may be of service to you.

While church members still wrestle with these issues, instruction is clear that Christians are to be active members in Christ's church by regularly meeting with other Christians. The example provided in the days following the resurrection of Jesus is to meet with a group of believers regularly and frequently for instruction, service, and fellowship.

The solution to deal with the imperfection of the world isn't to avoid church. The solution lies in the commitment to grow in a personal relationship with God by growing in knowledge of his word, with communication to him through prayer, fasting, and support from others with a genuine desire for a mature relationship with God. This requires obeying God's authority and an ever-growing reliance on him every day, all your life. And this includes active participation in church.

YOUR THOUGHTS?

- In what ways might fear be shown as an authority in a person's life?
- In what ways might selfishness be shown as an authority in a person's life?
- Have you ever been around a child or, for that matter, an adult who had no sense of obedience? If so, what destructive actions did you observe?
- How does obedience founded on love versus obedience founded on fear change one's view of obedience?
- How does faith affect a person's beliefs of obedience?
- What habits aid in the discipline of growing in obedience to God?
- Why do people attend church?
- What does Romans 6:16-18 state as the way out of being obedient to sin?
- What do Philippians 3:7-11 and 2 John 1:6 state about obedience to God?
- What does Galatians 5:13-26 state about a life led by God's spirit?

PART III
SOw WHAT ABOUT US

The need for help to live rightly leads us to the third part of this book. God allows us a relationship with him through the covenant that Jesus fulfilled with his death and resurrection for forgiveness of our sin. He didn't stop there. That is where your knowledge of who you are and your purpose for living begins.

Entering a relationship with God doesn't exempt you from temptations meant to separate you from him. Once saved, believers live through the journey of God positioning them toward his glory. Salvation doesn't mean we are perfect or without sin. We aren't immune to setbacks, pain, or tragedy. We will observe bad things happening to good people with little reason or consilience. Following God's ways will counter the world's ways. As such, we will experience conflict.

Thank God that he knows we will struggle. He has given us the power and guidance of the Holy Spirit. His Spirit is alive and part of our essence. While we can't avoid the pains of life, we can handle them much better. While we can't reason why certain things happen in this world, we can rely on him for strength of faith to learn more, rely more, and persevere. While hardship may be inevitable, we have God's unfailing love and power to help us to overcome doubt, pain, and death.

The presence of God is received as a personal relationship with him. It being personal gives us an understanding that God knows us, values us, and really does love us. God loves you and wants you to experience his excellence. And God guides us to his excellence with personal, practical, and doable instruction.

Part III provides instruction for several aspects of our character that promote relating with others in purposeful, fulfilling ways. God's word details how our speech so clearly defines our character. Maybe we need a deeper understanding of the essentialness of humility, faith, and forgiveness. Or perhaps we need reminded of the breath and power of God's love for us and what it means for us to follow his example by sharing his love with others.

🌱 8

LEAVING WORRY BEHIND

❧ FEAR-FULL OR FAITH-FULL

"Fear knocked at the door. Faith answered. And lo, no one was there." I don't know who came up with that truism, but it hits home with me. Maybe it is because of its conciseness or the clear contrast between fear and faith. Perhaps it is more. Maybe it reminds me of my continual personal struggle with fear.

I had the benefit of being raised around animals, mostly horses. We were in the business of producing and marketing them. Animals became my center of study in college and my career as a scientist. Animals, especially those that are highly reactive and intelligent as horses, are great teachers. And I fondly recall that they have taught me a lot about life.

Horses are the poster child of a noted behavior termed the fight-or-flight response. When facing an unknown or potentially harmful force, they characteristically respond by running away. As a handler, it serves your survival to be very aware of this instinct as you find yourself facing a thousand-pound animal with quick responses that can be detrimental to your well-being.

I fondly remember one young mare. She wasn't the best in the herd. She didn't have the good looks or athletic talent of her peers. But she taught me something no other has. Young horses tend to fear anything new, especially when surprised. Their response is usually a quick about-face, run, kick, buck, or other similarly amazing athletic response with little regard to a handler.

But she was different. When scared, she would stop briefly and then slowly move toward the focus of her fear. I can't tell you how odd that response was as I was conditioned as a handler for the opposite. She seemed to be in control of her actions when faced with the unknown.

I remember her at times I find myself fearful of the unknown. Sometimes overcoming the danger is as simple as keeping my cool while assessing the situation rather than running away or striking in anger. I'm not sure what she placed her faith in, if horses can have faith. Maybe it was in her abilities, be they less than her peers. Perhaps it was partially in her trust in me.

I'm often reminded of her example when I face fearful situations. I stop, reposition my thinking to get a better view, and try to understand the root of the fear. Moreover, I have found that my abilities are not enough. To be strong, I found the need for reliance on someone greater than me. And I thank God for being with me.

DON'T WORRY, BE HAPPY.

Anyone remember a song with that advice? Great advice, but it isn't easy to follow. Fear and the resultant worry are hardwired into our senses of self-preservation and control. As hard as we may try not to, we tend to respond to the unknown with fear and worry.

Worry and the resulting stress it brings are major health issues in the United States. Habitual worrying leads to physical and mental strain. Thoughts are guided habitually toward expecting the worst outcomes. Negative expectations reinforce negative actions, which lead to more negative expectations.

Our confidence turns into defeatism. Self-protection leads to isolation. Abilities turn into inabilities. Strength turns into weakness. Hopefully, this isn't a scenario that describes your present state of living. Unfortunately it is for most at some level and at some points in time.

God instructs us about worrying. Why do you suppose he is concerned about us worrying about life's issues? Worrying can be a sign of not trusting God. We place our trust in something else when we don't trust God. Sometimes we forget that he wants the best for us. He wants us to receive his blessings of protection, joy, confidence, and perseverance. As it is written in the book of Jeremiah, we receive the nourishment to overcome worry when we trust in God.

> But blessed is the one who trusts in the LORD, confidence is in him. They will be like a tree planted by the water sends out its roots by the stream. It does not fear when heat comes; leaves are always green. It has no worries in a year of drought and never fails to bear fruit. (Jeremiah 17:7–8)

Jesus told a relatable parable in the book of Luke. It speaks of the word of God as a seed.

> While a large crowd was gathering and people were coming to Jesus from town after town, he told this parable: "A farmer went out to sow his seed. As he was scattering the seed, some fell along the path; it was trampled on, and the birds ate it up. Some fell on rocky ground, and when it came up, the plants withered because they had no moisture. Other seed fell among thorns, which grew up with it and choked the plants. Still other seed fell on good soil. It came up and yielded a crop, a hundred times more than was sown."
>
> When he said this, he called out, "Whoever has ears to hear, let them hear." (Luke 8:4–9)

Jesus followed with the meaning of the parable in Luke 8:11–15. We don't receive God's word that falls among the thorns. We hear the word, yet our worries and misguided desires to define success in worldly terms choke our growth.

We know better. We've heard God's instruction. Even so, we often tend to move away from our source of nutrition and light. We fill with fear and despair when we don't receive the nourishment of his word.

~ FEAR

Where does the sense of worry come from? To generalize, worry comes from fear. We fear losing something or giving something away. We fear not measuring up to a self-imposed standard. We fear embarrassment and isolation if we reveal our imperfections to others.

Fear leads to a loss of personal, social, and spiritual growth. The sense of uselessness and helplessness born from fear leads in turn to a heightened sense of fear. We worry more and more about the unknown and uncontrollable. Our fear increases. The cycle of fear and worry can be vicious, consuming, and overwhelming, resulting in constant states of anxiety and depression.

~ STRENGTH TO WORRY NOT

Part of the answer to breaking the habit of worrying lies in overcoming the desire to worry. The desire to worry must be replaced with the desire to trust in someone who cares deeply for our well-being. As followers of Jesus, we know God loves us. And with that love, we have the strength of faith that God will help us overcome fear.

There are several benefits to overcoming the habit of worrying. While we may face the same issues, we work through them with new perspectives. Our goals broaden from avoidance or simply solving problems to our advantage to valuing the worth of the people involved in the circumstance. Combative environments turn into cooperative environments.

Our strength and confidence to overcome fear increase as our faith and reliance on God increases. We receive a sense of peace and strength to face future challenges. We can separate failures and successes from our belief in personal worth. We rely on God's belief in our worth when we fail. We praise God for his belief in our worth when we are successful.

The process of changing the habit of worry requires conscious effort on our part. It isn't easy and often not quickly or fully achieved. We must ask God for help to develop the mental discipline to fight and avoid the habit of worrying. Receiving counsel from Christians trained and experienced in helping others overcome worry can be very beneficial. They can help identify the real source of our worry.

It helps to recognize the source of our fear early in the process of responding to a situation or expectation. This may require us to face the issue early in its development and fight the desire to procrastinate mentally or physically. Above all, we must ask God for help and rely on his character for strength and hope.

Our ability to focus on God grows when we prioritize personal time with God through prayer, study of scripture, and fellowship with other Christians. When we rely on God, we are directed and strengthened by God. We do so by the gift of faith.

❧ FAITH

Usually people compartmentalize faith to the realms of belief in God. However, we place faith in many sources of authority. We place faith in families, friends, government, wealth, science, or laws of nature. We constantly place faith in objects we rely upon for support.

Use the example of automobiles. We place faith in the engineers, builders, and mechanics that vehicles will function to our need and favor. We place faith in those who are responsible for road design and maintenance to provide a safe path of travel.

We place faith in others to adhere to regulations and safe driving techniques that protect us. We place faith in our training, experience, and ability to operate the vehicle. These aren't trivial objects of faith considering we are moving such a heavy object at high rates of speed in extremely confining paths.

This trust defines whom or what has power and authority over us. Our trust goes beyond our comprehension of the source of our faith. Faith allows us to rely on what we don't understand with surety and certainty. Without faith, we live with an overwhelming sense of uncertainty and inconstancy. Lack of faith fosters our disbelief, doubt, and distrust in ourselves and others.

❧ FAITH IN GOD

As Christians, we believe in God's authority over everyone and everything. Our belief is he is all-powerful. We believe he is the ultimate authority for truth, justice, and mercy. We believe God is active in our lives. We believe his love for us is unfailing.

We don't limit our belief to what we can comprehend. We believe we don't have the ability to know everything about him. He is greater than us, and his ways are different than ours.

> Seek the Lord while he may be found; call on him while he is near. Let the wicked forsake their ways and the unrighteous their thoughts. Let them turn to the Lord, and he will have mercy on them, and to our God, for he will freely pardon. "For my thoughts are not your thoughts, neither are your ways my ways," declares the Lord. "As the heavens are higher than the earth, so are my ways higher than your ways and my thoughts than your thoughts." (Isaiah 55:6–9)

God's presence turns our disbelief into belief, confusion into clarity, doubt into confidence, and distrust into trust. Jesus's faith in us and our faith in Jesus provides this relationship, and the relationship is an ever-growing, continual process of revelation.

Belief is an integral part of faith. But faith has a greater meaning than simply believing. The meaning of the word faith is founded on the action of binding, or being drawn toward, as an action with a rope or cable. Our relationship with God is bound by faith. We bind our minds, hearts, and will to God. Seek God and he will draw you toward him.

~ GROWING IN FAITH

Some have the misunderstanding that Christian faith means never questioning God. We do, and he allows us to question. We have been given the gift of free will. Free will comes with curiosity and a desire to learn about the unknown. Our free will is directed toward what or whom we place our trust in and our faith upon. God intends free will to reinforce our desire to know more about truth, which is the same as desiring to know more about him.

God gives us just enough knowledge of truth so to encourage us to learn more about him, ourselves, and his creation. Like a staircase, we can move up a step, stand still with a firm foundation, and then move up a step. God created the universe in ways that give us reassurance and encouragement for living.

God gives us the linear nature of time so we can feel secure in our perceptions of past, present, and future. God created the world and, with it, his laws of nature we rely on for security. God gives us ability for awareness of the consistency of time and his laws of nature. We have faith they will be consistent and repetitive.

Some think we must separate God from growing in our knowledge of the world or more so believe that belief in science somehow requires disbelief in God. Nothing could be farther from the truth. Science provides the what and how of our world. God provides the why. Our belief in God strengthens the desire to understand his creation. Our world and all the principles that govern it were created by God for us. Our faith in God provides us the guidance and value to what we learn. "By faith we understand that the universe was formed at God's command, so that what is seen was not made out of what was visible" (Hebrews 11:3).

More about God and his creation is revealed as we practice and mature in our faith in him. This gradual process of revelation lessens the sense of being overwhelmed or insignificant by the enormity of what we don't understand. We can learn because he has given us the platform to advance in small steps knowing that our efforts won't end the need for further pursuit. Sounds like how we make advancements in science? Sounds like the revelation of God.

❧ LIVING IN FEAR OR FAITH

As followers of Jesus, we are attracted to God and desire to grow in our knowledge of him. However, we are immature and imperfect in that knowledge. Our immaturity allows fear to influence our thoughts, and our reasoning is based partially upon false presumptions. These presumptions hamper our growth.

Thankfully, we are given the gift of choosing a faith-led life. Faith provides the desire to be more: more purposeful, more knowledgeable, and more active in our service to God. Faith allows us to experience life abundantly, a life full of discovery, genuine relationships, and purpose.

So we have the will to mature by faith in God or to be stunted by a fear-filled spirit. Our influences, training, and actions will reinforce our direction toward one or the other. Our fear-filled spirit needs reinforcement. We have popularized made-up entities such as vampires and zombies. We celebrate customs such as Halloween to reinforce the feelings of release that come from being scared. Care must be taken to not elevate these feelings to a status of truth and authority. God warns about idolizing and false gods.

> We know also that the Son of God has come and has given us understanding, so that we may know him who is true. And we are in him who is true by being in his Son Jesus

Christ. He is the true God and eternal life.
Dear children, keep yourselves from idols.
(1 John 5:20–21)

On the other hand, insight gained from the Bible,
fellowship with followers of Jesus, prayer, instruction,
and obedience to God reinforce our faith-filled spirit. The
question is: which are you willing to reinforce, fear or faith?

❧ SCRIPTURAL REFERENCES FOR FAITH-FILLED LIVING

There is danger in providing examples of scripture that
relate to living a life guided by faith in God. The Bible is in
entirety a book of faith, and pulling excerpts does injustice
to the breath and importance of faith. Nonetheless, faith is
so important that the following are provided to stimulate
thought on the essentialness of faith and our need for
continual thanks to God for its gift.

By faith in Jesus

> … know that a person is not justified by the
> works of the law, but by faith in Jesus Christ.
> So we, too, have put our faith in Christ Jesus
> that we may be justified by faith in Christ
> and not by the works of the law, because by
> the works of the law no one will be justified.
> (Galatians 2:16)

> Consequently, faith comes from hearing the
> message, and the message is heard through
> the word about Christ. (Romans 10:17)

Right position with God

> For in the gospel the righteousness of God is revealed—a righteousness that is by faith from first to last, just as it is written: "The righteous will live by faith." (Romans 1:17)

> And without faith it is impossible to please God, because anyone who comes to him must believe that he exists and that he rewards those who earnestly seek him. (Hebrews 11:6)

Confidence and surety

> Now faith is confidence in what we hope for and assurance about what we do not see. (Hebrews 11:1)

Strength and protection

> But the Lord is faithful, and he will strengthen you and protect you from the evil one. (2 Thessalonians 3:3)

Healing

> Jesus turned and saw her. "Take heart, daughter," he said, "your faith has healed you." And the woman was healed at that moment. (Matthew 9:22)

Encouragement

> ... that is, that you and I may be mutually encouraged by each other's faith. (Romans 1:12)

> Therefore, brothers and sisters, in all our distress and persecution we were encouraged about you because of your faith. (1 Thessalonians 3:7)

Understanding

> By faith we understand that the universe was formed at God's command, so that what is seen was not made out of what was visible. (Hebrews 11:3)

Perseverance

> ... because you know that the testing of your faith produces perseverance. (James 1:3)

Forgiveness and salvation

> Some men brought to him a paralyzed man, lying on a mat. When Jesus saw their faith, he said to the man, "Take heart, son; your sins are forgiven." (Matthew 9:2)

> For it is by grace you have been saved, through faith—and this is not from yourselves, it is the gift of God. (Ephesians 2:8)

Growth in relationship with God

His master replied, "Well done, good and faithful servant! You have been faithful with a few things; I will put you in charge of many things. Come and share your master's happiness!" (Matthew 25:23)

YOUR THOUGHTS?

- Ten being at least once daily and one being less than once a week, how would you rate your frequency of consciously worrying about something?
- Do you think it is possible to develop a habit of worrying?
- How does fear play into worry?
- Are there times you find yourself worrying more than other times?
- Can worrying about something be beneficial?
- What are your first thoughts if asked to list three things you are most fearful of?
- Can fear be beneficial?
- When is fear most likely to occur?
- Amusement park rides are designed to enhance the feelings of fear and loss of control. Would you ride one that you had no faith in being safe?
- What does it take to grow in faith?
- How do trust and faith play into breaking a habit of worrying?
- Read the following Biblical passages. What thoughts come to mind about faith?

> Isaiah 55:6-9
> Galatians 2:16
> 1 John 5:20,21
> Ephesians 6:16
> Matthew 9:22
> James 1:3
> Matthew 25:23

🌱 9
SAY WHAT?

❧ REFLECTING ON A CAREER FILLED WITH PUBLIC SPEAKING

I spent a large part of my life communicating to individuals and groups via university outreach. Early on, as with most young go-getters, I was quick to provide recommendations on how I saw their needs. After all, that was what I did, as long as I had a sound basis for my information. And I had a lifetime of practical experience and three university degrees providing that sound basis.

Experience taught me a lot about communicating this knowledge. I found that many times what I said and what the people thought I said were different. Apparently, I assumed, they didn't follow me as closely as they should have. Or maybe they heard more of what they wanted to hear. Perhaps they really didn't care about what I was offering. Truth be told, I'm not nor ever was perfect in my abilities of communication. The result was a lot of miscommunication.

Looking back, my thirty-plus years of teaching could be divided into three almost equal phases. My early career presentations were focused on providing all the facts I could. And years of college and advanced degrees gave me a bunch. As I saw it, they needed all I could give them, especially the high-level stuff that made me sound smart.

The second phase centered on lowering the degree of information while increasing the impact of presentation. The advent of computer programs designed to enhance delivery took center stage. A picture did replace a thousand words in those multimedia presentations. Unfortunately, what that turned into was more concern about the picture and wowing the audiences with technology than concern on what they were hearing. What gains were made were joined with backward steps.

So although some may have thought I was becoming lazy in my preparation, I radicalized my approach in the last phase of my career. Most often, I would show up and start by providing just enough introduction about myself and the subject to gain the audience's trust to ask questions. And they had a lot of questions: questions related to what I had been billed to speak about and many off the subject. Listening and responding to their needs became the goal of my presentations.

It took a lot of guts on my part. Sometimes I had to admit that I didn't have the answers. Nonetheless, I found that the audiences were very attentive to what I saying. Likely that was because they were receiving a response to an inquiry rather than more information on the subject than they could grasp or for that matter wanted. And if the large number of follow-up requests for help were any indication, the people relied more on me afterward as a valued source of information.

I'm not sure what that says about my communication skills. Maybe listening was more important than talking.

Likely they knew more about what they needed than I did. Regardless, it wasn't as related as to how much I tried to wow them with knowledge or how polished the presentation, but more toward me as a trusted, objective, and caring person that understood their needs.

~❧ WHY TALK

Some people seem to talk way too much! We say, "They talk a lot about nothing" or "They must like to hear the sound of their own voice." Others seem to never say anything. We plead, "Just say something, anything!" And what are we to do with all those loud talkers, soft talkers, or those with an accent? I better stop, or I'll be accused of babbling.

Regardless of how we talk, we speak to cause a response. As Christians, we want that response to direct others to God's presence and advance his purpose. That requires us to continually receive a lot of instruction and guidance.

You won't read the Bible for very long before finding numerous accounts of how much our speech defines us. What we say, how we say it, and to whom we say it to may be the most defining pieces of our personality. God doesn't require everyone to speak in the same way. Some of us do talk too much, a few not enough, others too loudly, and several too softly, and all of us talk with an accent. God's instruction on speech directs us toward showing his character and away from speech that encourages temptation and sin.

◦ TO TELL THE TRUTH

Speaking the truth requires knowledge of truth and the desire to be led by that knowledge. God's word is truth. Jesus prays for this knowledge for us in his prayers before his death and resurrection, as written in John 17.

While most people believe telling the truth is best, it isn't always so easy. What circumstances might pressure you to lie? To save someone else from harm? To attempt to save yourself from harm? To gain something thought unattainable by the truth? We are plainly instructed to speak the truth.

> "These are the things you are to do: Speak the truth to each other, and render true and sound judgment in your courts; do not plot evil against each other, and do not love to swear falsely. I hate all this," declares the Lord. (Zechariah 8:16–17)

The preceding scripture also teaches against loving to swear falsely. What comes to mind when you hear the word *swear*? Today, we may relate it only to cursing. Swearing is actually appealing for God's truth to be affirmed. For example, a jury is sworn in to seek and make decisions based on truth. A witness is sworn in to tell the truth. In the past, these declarations were done with a person's hand on a Bible.

Is there danger in telling the truth? Likely so, if it negatively affects those who don't want to hear the truth. You may feel like an enemy to the very people you are trying to help, as with Paul and the people of Galatia. Paul pleads for them to follow Christ at a time they were being taught false doctrines on the gift of salvation. In Galatians 4:16, he poses the question, "Have I now become your enemy by telling you the truth?"

A word of caution is in order. Speaking the truth is received most effectively when a person is open to it. We must be aware that grief, pain, and anger, although hopefully temporary conditions, are real. During these times, it may be best to hold your speech. As the author of the book of James states,

> My dear brothers and sisters, take note of this: Everyone should be quick to listen, slow to speak and slow to become angry, because human anger does not produce the righteousness that God desires (James 1:19–20).

While this may be hard to do for all my fellow problem-solving personalities, it is best. Too many times, we are drawn into confrontation and end up stating positions that are not founded on the truth of the matter. Like the friends mentioned in the book of Job, maybe the wisest course would heed to Job's request, "If only you would be altogether silent! For you, that would be wisdom" (Job 13:5).

His friends thought they were offering helpful advice founded on truth. They weren't. Good intentions weren't much of an excuse for what turned bantering back and forth. Maybe the more correct action would have been to listen to Job and to pray for Job's recovery and comfort. Reasoning the cause or offering self-formulated solutions for relief was not what Job needed. It would have been best if they had heeded Job's request.

Contrarily, staying silent or being slow to speak shouldn't be motivated by denying Jesus or loving something else more. It should be motivated by the opposite, a desire to show the supremacy of Jesus's worth and love in our lives.

❧ NO LIE

It should follow that we are not to lie, and the Bible is full of instruction to not. Consider the following verses of scripture:

> Whoever of you loves life and desires to see many good days, keep your tongue from evil and your lips from telling lies. (Psalm 34:12–13)

> Do not lie to each other, since you have taken off your old self with its practices and have put on a new self, which is being renewed in knowledge in the image of its Creator. (Colossians 3:9–10)

> Therefore each of you must put off falsehood and speak truthfully to your neighbor, for we are all members of one body. (Ephesians 4:25)

Who do you define to be your neighbor? In no way would it be implied it is ok to lie to your non-neighbors. How does a sense of loving life counter the desire to use speech for evil? Does the assurance of being renewed in knowledge in the image of God give you hope that you can avoid the temptation to lie?

❧ USELESS AND HARMFUL SPEECH

The Bible also provides many warnings about bad speech. Some of the common issues are addressed. You may have others to add to the list. Define the issue before thinking about the message of the verses. Whereas something like idleness seems easy to understand, others such as flattery, slander, and blasphemy may be more difficult.

Complaining

> Do everything without grumbling or arguing, so that you may become blameless and pure, "children of God without fault in a warped and crooked generation." Then you will shine among them like stars in the sky as you hold firmly to the word of life. (Philippians 2:14–16)

This speech should be easy to recognize. We complain to express grief, pain, or uneasiness or to accuse another of an offense. Complaining seems to be an integral part of our psyche. Nothing new for Christians, the Bible is full of complainers: complaining about circumstances in life, complaining about others, and complaining to God.

We seem to unconsciously complain from the time we wake up to the time we sleep. I'm not sure why we are so quick to focus on the negative. Maybe it's part of shirking the responsibility to make things better. Perhaps it's satisfying or validating for someone else to hear our troubles. It could be a way to show how proudful we think of ourself. Maybe we do it to relieve stress. Most likely, it's just for attention and an attempt to fill some emptiness in us.

Psychologists point out that the root of the problem is often different than the focus of the complaint, especially for chronic complainers. And while complaining may be done to relieve stress, it can add to it. While we may complain for validation, it may lessen our validity of what others think of us.

We did an exercise with a group of youth to emphasize how often we complain without thinking about it. They were asked up-front how often they complained during a twenty-four-hour period. We had them wear a rubber band on their wrist, and they were asked to flick the band every time they caught themselves complaining. Using the buddy system helped with accountability. Even within an hour into the exercise, they found all had significantly underestimated their frequency of complaining. I had to ask one to remove the rubber band because of the bruises she was causing on her wrist.

It takes a conscious effort and a lot of help to curb complaining. Maybe wearing a rubber band on your wrist is one way to bring it to focus. But long-term behavior adjustment will take more than a rubber band. It will take help from the giver of life, Jesus, guidance from the Holy Spirit, and a desire to become more Christ-light in your nature.

Perverse and corrupt speech

> Keep your mouth free of perversity; keep corrupt talk far from your lips. (Proverbs 4:24)

Perverse speech is done to twist and distort what is right, hence to distort the righteousness of God. Corrupt speech is simply speech that is dishonest or immoral. From my experience, those who consistently use perverse and corrupt speech most often try to elicit a reaction to move others from what is right, honest, and moral. The shocking nature of perverse and corrupt speech can be a tempting lure to encourage a listener to move toward similar actions. Again, the cause likely comes from seeking attention to fill an emptiness within. Or, as times my grandmother was admonishing me, cursing, perverse, and corrupt speech may simply be an expression of a lazy mind.

I've also wondered why we tend to allow perversity and corrupt speech in adults while not allowing it in children. Is it a privilege for being a grown-up? Are we better at using it as adults only when we deem it appropriate? When would it be appropriate? Seems like childish behavior to me.

Even the use of the word *adult* in tags of businesses and media, for instance, adult bookstore or adult audiences only, is an interesting juxtaposition. It seems like the glorification of perverse and corrupt speech would be too childish than what should be defined as adult behavior.

Flattery and boasting

> May the Lord silence all flattering lips and every boastful tongue—those who say, "By our tongues we will prevail; our own lips will defend us—who is lord over us?" (Psalm 12:3–4)

So what's the big deal with a little flattery? Doesn't it make the person feel good? To answer those questions, you must define flattery. You are experiencing false praise when you give or receive flattery. Maybe it is done with a good intention of making a person feel better. But flattery is usually done to gain attention and influence. And when discovered, it's insulting to the person to think the giver's intent could fool them.

Boasting is a little less acceptable in our societies. Boasting is done to glorify oneself. Those who boast about themselves separate their abilities from God's authority. In my experience, the need to boast results when there is a feeling of inadequacy in a time of competitiveness.

> This is what the Lord says: "Let not the wise boast of their wisdom or the strong boast of their strength or the rich boast of their riches, but let the one who boasts boast about this: that they have the understanding to know me, that I am the Lord, who exercises kindness, justice and righteousness on earth, for in these I delight," declares the Lord. (Jerimiah 9:23–24)

Gossip

> Besides, they get into the habit of being idle and going about from house to house. And not only do they become idlers, but also busybodies who talk nonsense, saying things they ought not to. (1 Timothy 5:13)

The *they* referred to in the above verse are "younger widows." But don't begin to think any age group, sex, or other delineation of humanity doesn't gossip. Why the need? Maybe we gossip to feel important or to gain intimacy. That's a shame because the receiving person will have less confidence in the relationship for fear of being the next person to be gossiped about.

Maybe we gossip with a good intent of warning others about the focus of the gossip. Unfortunately, most of those situations quickly turn into judgmental comments. Maybe it results from idleness and boredom. If that's the case, we need to avoid idleness and boredom.

So is there a real issue with gossiping or spreading nonsense? Usually yes. As Scripture states, we likely underestimate the impact on those receiving gossip. "The words of a gossip are like choice morsels; they go down to the inmost parts" (Proverbs 26:22).

Gossiping also causes the listener to join into something that was stated in confidence. Increases in conflict and quarreling result.

> A gossip betrays a confidence; so avoid anyone who talks too much. (Proverbs 20:19).

> Without wood a fire goes out; without a gossip a quarrel dies down. (Proverbs 26:20)

Slander

> Do not go about spreading slander among your people. Do not do anything that endangers your neighbor's life. I am the Lord. (Leviticus 19:16)

Slander occurs when a person spreads false information about others to tarnish their reputations. We usually give the need to avoid slander more credence than flattery or boasting. Maybe it's the potential of a legal suit against a slanderer. The basis for legal action results from loss of livelihood or status by the false reports. While we can understand the instruction to not slander, the instruction to answer kindly when slandered is a little hard to take. "When we are slandered, we answer kindly. We have become the scum of the earth, the garbage of the world— right up to this moment" (1 Corinthians 4:13).

Paul was writing this letter (1 Corinthians) to the church to document how the apostles responded to the slander they endured as followers of Jesus. Using irony, Paul was admonishing the church member's actions of selfishness. Suffering for the sake of Christ can make us feel like we are seen as the scum of the earth. Maybe that isn't all bad, especially when we look to what the world offers for acceptance and validation. Scum on the surface of water may look gross, but at least it usually is positioned above the rest of the water.

Blasphemy

> You shall not misuse the name of the LORD your God, for the LORD will not hold anyone guiltless who misuses his name. (Exodus 20:7)

This moves up the scale of avoidance, even for those unsure of their relationship with God. Blasphemy is done to injure God. It includes speech that denies God what is due to him and stating attributes about God that aren't agreeable to his nature. That opens a world of thought on the importance of carefully guarding speech and the need to seek forgiveness for sin.

∿ SPEAK WITH A PURPOSE

Some of us like to talk. Others would rather not talk. Whether we dilute our speech with many words or give out super-concentrated doses of wisdom doesn't matter as much as our purpose for speaking. Consider the following, "The mouths of the righteous utter wisdom, and their tongues speak what is just. The law of his God is in his heart; his feet do not slip" (Psalm 37:30–31).

How do you know you are uttering wisdom and speaking what is just? It starts the definition of wisdom. From a Christian perspective, wisdom is seen as sound judgment when attempting good or countering evil. Sound judgment requires knowledge and respect of God, guidance from the Holy Spirit, and genuine effort to obey God's commands.

A few examples of how we are to guide our speech follow. Reflect on times you've experienced instances that relate to the following verses. Any verses hard for you to live out? What advice could you give a friend who is struggling with one of the issues brought up in the following verses?

> Preach the word; be prepared in season and out of season; correct, rebuke and encourage—with great patience and careful instruction. For the time will come when men will not put up with sound doctrine. Instead, to suit their own desires, they will gather around them a great number of teachers to say what their itching ears want to hear. They will turn their ears away from the truth and turn aside to myths. (2 Timothy 4:2–5)

Don't let anyone look down on you because you are young, but set an example for the believers in speech, in conduct, in love, in faith and in purity. (1 Timothy 4:12)

A gentle answer turns away wrath, but a harsh word stirs up anger. (Proverbs 15:1)

Fools show their annoyance at once, but the prudent overlook an insult. (Proverbs 12:16)

ENCOURAGE OTHERS

Do not let any unwholesome talk come out of your mouths, but only what is helpful for building others up according to their needs, that it may benefit those who listen. (Ephesians 4:29)

This subsection could easily have been included in the preceding discussion of speaking with a purpose. But in my opinion, it bears more significance. Worldly influences most often offer discouragement. Those who have little hope and faith seek comfort by discouraging others. Most of us, when aware, will be given many opportunities to encourage others. Yet so many times, we don't act upon opportunities to encourage another who may be disheartened, unsure, or fearful.

Simply defined, encourage means to give courage to another. So why isn't encouragement more of a staple of our speech? First, to give courage means you must have courage: courage to give something to someone with no interest to self or expectation of return. That's hard. We tend to think ourselves as receivers of gifts more so than givers.

Second, real encouragement involves investment into another's issues. As the verse above states, "according to their needs," we need to listen to the person before genuinely and knowledgeably respond with encouragement. The encouragement we receive from God strengthens us to encourage others.

> May our Lord Jesus Christ himself and God our Father, who loved us and by his grace gave us eternal encouragement and good hope, encourage your hearts and strengthen you in every good deed and word. (2 Thessalonians 2:16–17)

YOUR THOUGHTS?

- When was the last time you said something that afterward wished you hadn't?
- When was the last time you didn't say something that afterward wished you had?
- When was the last time you felt you were having a hard time being understood?
- When do you feel most at ease to speak to someone?
- When do you feel least comfortable speaking to someone?
- Are there certain topics you find yourself talking about a lot?
- Are there certain topics you don't want to talk about?
- What instruction is provided from the following Biblical passages?

> Colossians 3:9,10
> Philippians 2:14-16
> Proverbs 4:24
> Psalm 12:3,4
> Proverbs 26:22
> Exodus 20:7
> Psalm 37:30,31
> 2 Timothy 4:2-5
> Ephesians 4:29

🌱 10
HUMBLY STRONG

❧ DRAWN TO THE HUMBLE

Unfortunately some people think that in order to be humble, you must dwell on your shortcomings and how much you don't measure up. In this manner, humility would promote an excuse to draw back from challenges and keep you from succeeding in our competitive world. Being humble would have the connotation of being weak, not strong.

I find all that untrue as I reflect on the people I have most admired as mentors. Humility is about focusing on the needs and abilities of others rather than your own. That position is different than believing you are less valuable to God than someone else. Focusing on others' needs requires strength, not weakness.

I remember a father of a close high school friend who had that inner strength. He was very successful but didn't let that success overpower who he was or what he wanted to represent. I found myself at their house as often as possible and was sure to listen when he spoke.

My college career was filled with many professorial

advisors. There were two or three that greatly impacted my life. Yes, they were top in their knowledge of their technical field. But moreover, they seemed to respect students and prioritized our growth over the need for self-glorification. I was quick to take their advice when they offered direction.

And as a professor, I found an older coworker so well respected that three generations of past students kept in touch with him following his retirement and later collectively grieved his passing at his funeral. We knew his suggestions for conducting the many diverse activities we faced were well thought out and motivated for the good of all. We listened, learned, and gained valuable perspectives from him.

All these people had individual talents and strengths. All had different levels of success as measured by the world's standards. But all had great strength with humility. They were able to define and hold to their beliefs no matter the situation. Their actions went beyond the goal of self-advancement and personal glory.

There was an internal strength in these men that didn't require self-promotion, advancement by selfish actions, or claims to credit for the actions of others. There was something solid about how their *internalness* exemplified a sense of eternalness. Their confidence in truth made them humbly strong.

WORLDVIEW OF HUMILITY

A comedian brought up an interesting point of view. Part of our definition of a hero is that a hero must be humble. Think about it. The football game comes down to the last play. A player, who has fought through injury, fights to the end. The last play begins. The player makes a superhuman catch. He runs through the defense, bouncing off would-be tacklers. Even the opposing fans are amazed at his play. Never has anything like it been seen or expected to be seen again. Touchdown is scored. Victory comes with the last play! It is obvious who was to receive MVP honors.

The player is interviewed afterward. The leading question from reporters is, "How does it feel to be the MVP?" Now, you fill in his answer. How about "Of course I won MVP. Hadn't you been watching? What did you expect? No one is as good as me. I'm better injured than they are healthy. This team wouldn't be anything without me."

That answer doesn't sit too well with our desire to hero-worship. We go away thinking, *Oh man, he sure is talented, but what an ego! Let someone else buy his jersey. I want no part of it or him, his team, or what he represents.* As the comedian presented, our heroes must be humble. But does being humble require you to display timidity? When does confidence turn into arrogance?

We all struggle with humility, confidence, and arrogance. Humility can be perceived as being meek, submissive, and mild. These traits are not admired in our world's view of success, individualism, and competition. Confidence is more admired because of the associated displays of courage, assurance, and boldness. Conversely confidence in one's abilities can lead to arrogance and with it an overestimation of importance and ability.

From afar, it is easy to view those with humble personalities as weak. But with closer relationships, true humility becomes admired and seen as strength. Humility positions one to receive and provide advice, which increases the knowledge to handle situations. Humility increases consistency in behavior and objectivity in decision-making. Humility encourages focus on accomplishing a goal rather than the need for drawing attention to oneself. Approachability, a source of objectivity, a trusted source for advice, and an ability to accomplish goals are desirable traits for anyone's definition of MVP.

We define confidence as feeling certain about a fact or the truth. What may be seen as confidence at first impression may be later identified as arrogance. Feeling assured of one's own abilities can lead to having an exaggerated sense of one's importance or abilities. The air of confidence then becomes filled with the stench of conceit. People isolate themselves from those viewed as arrogant. The exchange of information is incomplete, untrusted, and biased. Miscommunication prevails. The result is an arrogant or conceited person winds up with less importance and abilities over time.

⮞ HUMILITY EMPOWERED BY GOD

A Christian's sense of humility and confidence comes from a relationship with God. Having a relationship with him is incomprehensible. We are not worthy to have it, yet Jesus gave us that relationship as a gift through his birth, life, death, and resurrection. There is nothing we can do to earn it, and although we continue to rebel against God, we are forgiven. His love is unfailing. Our worth is in our acceptance of the love of Jesus Christ.

Jesus, God incarnated, came to serve, and give his life as a ransom for many (Mark 10:45). We have gained freedom over death and the power of sin (Romans 8:1-3).

We are to use that freedom to serve one another humbly in love (Galatians 5:13).

God's righteousness brings us peace; its effect is quietness and confidence forever (Isaiah 32:17). With the help of God's Spirit and the example of Jesus, we gain confidence in God's authority, protection, and love. We find that humility is not thinking less of ourselves. Humility gives of the strength to think of ourselves less and the needs of others more.

While we may willingly approach God with a humble spirit, we may struggle more with humbly approaching others. We tend to elevate our value above others because of our competitive nature, sense of pride, or feeling of self-importance. We judge our worth in comparison with the worth of those around us. Further, we measure the worth of others with our self-defined worth of ourselves.

By doing so, we base our worth and the worth of others on imperfection. That results in a perception of worth based on relativity of the comparison. With relativity, we lose confidence in the surety of our and others' value. We lose our focus on God's righteousness and Jesus's example, and in doing so, lose the peace, quietness, and confidence that results. When we do, we tend to build up a defense of arrogance.

❧ STRUGGLING WITH ARROGANCE

The temptation for arrogance, egotism, and selfishness is a part of all lives. Sometimes it is plainly obvious. Other times, we display a false sense of humility to gain stature among our peers. We tend to sense arrogance more when we are actively engaged with people. So is it best to simply isolate ourselves from others so we avoid the temptation of being arrogant? Is lack of interaction the only way to be humble? Or does interaction only bring to light what is already there?

God doesn't desire us to believe sin has power over him or his desires for us. He desires us to have relationships and to be a positive influence to others. Humility doesn't hamper the ability to relate with or to be an influence on others. Rather it is essential. There is little doubt in the historical significance of Moses as a leader. An entire people group followed his influence for many decades. When chosen by God, Moses quickly refuted his ability to lead.

> Moses said to the Lord, "Pardon your servant, Lord. I have never been eloquent, neither in the past nor since you have spoken to your servant. I am slow of speech and tongue." (Exodus 4:10)

God's reply and anger that followed admonished Moses for his lack of reliance on him. It wasn't Moses's perception of personal skills that made him a desirable leader. God was directing Moses to be confident in the truth. God was able to use Moses as a leader of his people because of Moses' faith and, with that faith, Moses' humbleness. This is revealed plainly in a single verse in parentheses in the book of Numbers when others questioned Moses's relationship with God.

> (Now Moses was a very humble man, more humble than anyone else on the face of the earth.) (Numbers 12:3)

~♥ HUMILITY TO GOD FIRST AND FOREMOST

Receiving God's care and love does not mean we won't struggle with self-reliance and arrogance. There are numerous biblical accounts of these struggles among leaders. The book of 2 Chronicles repeatedly documents successes and failures of kings of God's chosen people. Those who acknowledged their errors or arrogance humbled themselves before God and were brought back into a relationship with him. Consider King Manasseh.

> In his distress he sought the favor of the LORD his God and humbled himself greatly before the God of his ancestors. And when he prayed to him, the LORD was moved by his entreaty and listened to his plea; so he brought him back to Jerusalem and to his kingdom. Then Manasseh knew that the LORD is God. (2 Chronicles 33:12–13)

Those who didn't acknowledge their position with God with humility met other fates. Consider Manasseh's son, Amon.

> But unlike his father Manasseh, he did not humble himself before the LORD; Amon increased his guilt. Amon's officials conspired against him and assassinated him in his palace. (2 Chronicles 33:23–24)

God has provided many biblical references as warnings against arrogance. A few examples follow.

"See, I am against you, you arrogant one,"
declares the Lord, the Lord Almighty, "for
your day has come, the time for you to be
punished." (Jeremiah 50:31)

Before a downfall the heart is haughty, but
humility comes before honor. (Proverbs 18:12)

Haughty eyes and a proud heart—the
unplowed field of the wicked—produce sin.
(Proverbs 21:4)

Why do you suppose God is so adamant about correcting
arrogance? The quick answer is arrogance separates us
from God. He loves us and wants us to experience his
excellence. And he wants to equip us to show others that
excellence.

Our reverence to God positions us to be humble.
The more we understand and submit to his authority
and power, the more we are humbled. The more we
understand his desire and love for us, the more we are
humbled. Our humbleness is reflected from the strength
of our reliance on God's power and authority. It can't be
genuine, sustained, or produced by any other power. God
desires us to be humble and plainly instructs us on his
provisions for the humble.

... if my people, who are called by my name,
will humble themselves and pray and seek
my face and turn from their wicked ways,
then I will hear from heaven, and I will
forgive their sin and will heal their land. (2
Chronicles 7:14)

He mocks proud mockers but shows favor to the humble and oppressed. (Proverbs 3:34)

He guides the humble in what is right and teaches them his way. (Psalm 25:9)

The Lord sustains the humble but casts the wicked to the ground. (Psalm 147:6)

For the Lord takes delight in his people; he crowns the humble with victory. (Psalm 149:4)

The greatest among you will be your servant. For those who exalt themselves will be humbled, and those who humble themselves will be exalted. (Matthew 23:11-12)

No doubt we will struggle with arrogance, egotism, and humility no matter how closely aligned we are to God's appointment and purpose for our lives. This struggle even may be more evident in times we are most active in our passion for God. The more we are empowered to influence others, the more we must rely on God's strength rather than our own and the more we should profess him to others rather than crediting ourselves.

YOUR THOUGHTS?

- Do you view people with a humble personality as mentally or physically weak?
- Conversely, is arrogance viewed as mentally or physically strong?
- What can humility open you up to?
- What is the difference between confidence and arrogance?
- What can arrogance open you up to?
- Does humility restrict the desire to act on issues you are passionate about?
- Does arrogance restrict the desire to act on issues you are passionate about?
- What instruction is provided from the following Biblical passages?

    Proverbs 18:12
    2 Chronicles 7:14
    Matthew 23:12
    Psalm 25:9
    2 Chronicles 7:14

🌱 11
FORGIVEN AND FORGIVING

∽ FORGETTING TO FORGIVE?

I have a confession. I have a problem with forgiving others. Somehow, I have gone through life believing we are responsible for ourselves and our actions and, when one messes up, above all one must pay the consequences. And consequences are final. Maybe it is a sense of justice or an inherent emptiness of mercy or overfill of selfishness. While I may tolerate someone harming me or someone else, forgiveness is another matter. My thought is it isn't my responsibility to forgive. I wasn't the one who committed the offense.

Oh, that doesn't mean I won't forgive people for an unintentional assault or a little thing. After all, I reason that I've been guilty of those situations. It's the big things I struggle with, the ones that caused great harm and loss I won't consider forgiving. Some things are so bad that a person should live with the offense forever, and my unforgiveness somehow solidifies their guilt and my innocence. Moreover, some things are too big to forget, and if I can't forget, they shouldn't be forgiven.

Over time, I'm finding the logic for the above thoughts to be false. Forgetting is not part of the definition of forgiveness. Determining who does and doesn't deserve forgiveness is confusing. For example, I might be willing to forgive my child for an offense I wouldn't for someone else's child. And how does my forgiving someone disprove their guilt or prove my innocence?

Fortunately I have God's testament in Jesus to direct my thoughts and beliefs of forgiveness. His gift of forgiveness gives me the strength to live in a world full of pain, injustice, and immorality and, by his example, the strength to forgive others.

I thank God for forgiving me and having patience as I struggle with forgiveness. I've been given what I didn't deserve: God's forgiveness of my trespasses on others and him. Maybe it's time I grow up and rely on his example for strength to forgive.

∾ DESIRING FORGIVENESS

We may desire to be forgiven and to forgive, but being empowered to do so is a different story. We remember trespasses. We live in a world full of people who commit unfair acts. Forgiveness counters our sense of justice.

So is it as easy as forgive and forget? What if you can't forget? Does that mean you don't have to forgive? Unless we undergo brain surgery, forgetting can be impossible. But what about forgiving? Is forgiveness and forgetting the same thing?

Our senses of personal survival and societal fairness promote us to hold onto hurtful, unfair acts we've received in the past. Fair play suggests that whoever is responsible should at the least receive the same level of hurt they gave. This sense of fair play goes both ways, unfair acts we commit or receive.

After all, isn't an eye for an eye a logical way to control the rules of a relationship? That may seem so in the immediate. The long-term result of that logic is the darkness that results from more and more eyes being lost. Holding onto an offense brings anger and bitterness into relationships past, present, and future. Its grip promotes isolation, anxiousness, and depression.

Moving beyond the thought of being victimized releases the power and control past injustices have on our lives. It doesn't mean that the offense received was fair. Similarly, releasing guilt we hold from committing injustices will also lessen the power and control they have on our lives. That bears restating. We must get past the hold offenses have on our lives regardless of our thoughts of fairness.

∾ PAST FAIR

We generally categorize offenses we receive as unfair. Take the example of missing the boat. Have you ever been denied access to something because of a missed deadline or tardiness? Maybe this occurred with no ill intention on your part. Perhaps there was a traffic jam caused by someone standing in the middle of the road. Fair that you were delayed? Maybe not. Fair that the deadline was imposed anyway? Maybe so. Maybe no.

We must be very careful not to confuse right and fair. Our definition of fairness is skewed toward our position and viewpoint. Our judgment of fairness is conditional to how we are affected. And blaming others for their position can elevate your self-justification of innocence. Simply, our thoughts of fair and unfair are subjective.

On the other hand, God determines what is right. We see righteousness in his perfect, all-powerful, and unchanging character. Being right isn't about positioning blame for an offense. It is more about our response to unfair acts. Following God's instruction and guidance positions us to respond rightly to unfair situations. Our goal should be to respond righteously rather than dwelling on the need for judgment of fairness.

A past ice storm caused a multi-day power outage across the state. People were responding to service providers in a variety of ways, some positive and others negative. Those who received power quickly expressed relief and thanks. Many who didn't were quick to blame the inequity of the provider's response and state the unfairness of the situation. Loss of control brought out many accusations and much anger.

One provider was sharing his experiences and commenting how positive I was about waiting as compared with many others. I could have blamed the unpreparedness of the responders. I could have been angry that we weren't the first to receive attention. There was a lot about the whole mess that could be expressed as unfair.

I accepted that I wasn't in control of the situation. I was, however, responsible for how I responded to it. Granted, I had similar thoughts of the unfairness of the response time and not being one of the first to receive service. For the most part, I chose to not let those thoughts or the situation define who I was then or would be in the future. After all, I hope to have to live with myself for many years to come. My desire to seek righteous behavior outweighed my natural instincts centered on myself.

Several past coworkers have at times become so consumed with what their boss or the system has done to them that their entire personality centers around those thoughts of injustice. I've had the opportunity to counsel some with hopes they would see just how much power the opposing entity had on them. In essence, it has consumed them.

They were existing only as a reflection of what they detested. Their identity became a product of their dissatisfaction. Their need for retribution consumed their desire and power to move past the grip it held on them. What was needed most was the power to forgive.

❧ POWER TO FORGIVE

Forgiveness releases the power that unfair acts have on you. That requires a commitment on your part to a process of change. As you let go of grudges, you will no longer be defined only by how you've been hurt. Letting go of bitterness opens you up to healthier relationships, less anxiety, and higher self-esteem. It isn't easy, and we don't have the self-power to do so.

The power to forgive comes from the one who has forgiven beyond our comprehension. God desires us to be forgiven and to forgive others. His actions and instruction help us define the basis and path of forgiveness.

> For if you forgive other people when they sin against you, your heavenly Father will also forgive you. But if you do not forgive others

their sins, your Father will not forgive your
sins. (Matthew 6:14–15)

And when you stand praying, if you hold
anything against anyone, forgive them, so
that your Father in heaven may forgive you
your sins. (Mark 11:25)

God knows the difficulty we have with desiring to forgive
others for their wrongdoings. Personal sacrifice doesn't
come easily or naturally. Scripture provides instruction to
help us place forgiveness into action.

Get rid of all bitterness, rage and anger,
brawling and slander, along with every form
of malice. Be kind and compassionate to
one another, forgiving each other, just as in
Christ God forgave you. (Ephesians 4:31–32)

Do not say, "I'll do to them as they have
done to me; I'll pay them back for what they
did." (Proverbs 24:29)

Then Peter came to Jesus and asked, "Lord,
how many times shall I forgive my brother
or sister who sins against me? Up to seven
times?" Jesus answered, "I tell you, not seven
times, but seventy-seven times." (Matthew
18:21–22)

∾ FORGIVING ISN'T EASY

We desire God and understand that his purpose for us is the answer to our pursuit of fulfillment. His forgiveness gives us the gift of life. Even with his example, forgiving others isn't easy. We may forgive someone for an accidental, temporary hurt. We find ourselves saying something like "No big deal," "I know you are sorry," "You didn't mean it," or "It was nothing at all."

But someone committing an intentional, deep, irreversible injury for no reason other than what we perceive as evil isn't easy to forgive. Moreover, we feel little responsibility to do so. We have no desire to do so. We find ourselves saying something like, "There are just some things to heinous to forgive." We judge which trespasses are too large for forgiveness.

Scripture provides an abundance of warnings to avoid arrogance, retribution, judgment, and intolerance. These traits place us out of position with God's character and, by doing so, limit our power and desire to forgive. Consider the following scriptures:

> Woe to those who are wise in their own eyes and clever in their own sight. (Isaiah 5:21)

> Do not repay anyone evil for evil. Be careful to do what is right in the eyes of everyone. If it is possible, as far as it depends on you, live at peace with everyone. Do not take revenge, my dear friends, but leave room for God's wrath, for it is written: "It is mine to avenge; I will repay," says the Lord. On the contrary: "If your enemy is hungry, feed

him; if he is thirsty, give him something to drink. In doing this, you will heap burning coals on his head." Do not be overcome by evil, but overcome evil with good. (Romans 12:17–21)

Do not judge, or you too will be judged. For in the same way you judge others, you will be judged, and with the measure you use, it will be measured to you. Why do you look at the speck of sawdust in your brother's eye and pay no attention to the plank in your own eye? How can you say to your brother, "Let me take the speck out of your eye," when all the time there is a plank in your own eye? You hypocrite, first take the plank out of your own eye, and then you will see clearly to remove the speck from your brother's eye. (Matthew 7:1–5)

❧ GOD FILLS THE NEED

So where does the power to forgive come from? I think any Christian would answer God to that question. The power to forgive depends on filling yourself with the character of God. God's teachings emphasize the necessity of love as the foundation of forgiveness.

Do not conform to the pattern of this world, but be transformed by the renewing of your mind. Then you will be able to test and approve what God's will is—his good, pleasing and perfect will. (Romans 12:2)

Hatred stirs up conflict, but love covers over all wrongs. (Proverbs 10:12)

Do not seek revenge or bear a grudge against anyone among your people, but love your neighbor as yourself. I am the LORD. (Leviticus 19:18)

If you love those who love you, what credit is that to you? Even sinners love those who love them. And if you do good to those who are good to you, what credit is that to you? Even sinners do that. And if you lend to those from whom you expect repayment, what credit is that to you? Even sinners lend to sinners, expecting to be repaid in full. But love your enemies, do good to them, and lend to them without expecting to get anything back. Then your reward will be great, and you will be children of the Most High, because he is kind to the ungrateful and wicked. Be merciful, just as your Father is merciful. (Luke 6:32–36)

As Colossians 3:12–14 states, God instructs us to clothe ourselves with compassion, kindness, humility, gentleness, and patience. As we do, others see those traits in us. These traits, prayed for, practiced, and obtained, align us with God's character. These virtues are bound with love. Love is the basis for the power and desire to forgive others. As with all struggles in life, it isn't as simple as turning away from a harmful emotion or thought. We must move toward God. And the first step is to ask and accept his forgiveness of your sins.

~ SEEKING FORGIVENESS

Asking your forgiveness from others you may have harmed may be more difficult than forgiving others. I've done things that have hurt others that were motivated intentionally through my selfishness. At the time, fear, pride, hurt, and the need to retaliate clouded my vision. Looking back, I am more able to see the situation objectively.

It is hard, but I've asked forgiveness from some I've wronged. The hardest part was being honest with myself and building the courage to ask. Responses have been variable. Some didn't remember the offense to be as large as I had made it out to be. A few didn't remember the offense at all. It was obvious that others were still angry about it. Regardless of the level of acceptance, I felt closer to God. Our relationship with God is strengthened when we settle quarrels or differences.

> Therefore, if you are offering your gift at the altar and there remember that your brother or sister has something against you, leave your gift there in front of the altar. First go and be reconciled to them; then come and offer your gift. (Matthew 5:23–24)

❧ THE GOOD AND BAD OF SORROW

Great sorrow can come from unforgiveness, but sorrow can fuel our ability to seek or give forgiveness. Sorrow can produce good or bad paths. It is harmful if it leads to isolation from God's authority The apostle Paul defines this as worldly sorrow in his letter to the church in Corinth. Sorrow can lead us to ask God for forgiveness through confession and repentance. Paul defines this as godly sorrow.

Even if I caused you sorrow by my letter, I do not regret it. Though I did regret it—I see that my letter hurt you, but only for a little while—yet now I am happy, not because you were made sorry, but because your sorrow led you to repentance. For you became sorrowful as God intended and so were not harmed in any way by us. Godly sorrow brings repentance that leads to salvation and leaves no regret, but worldly sorrow brings death. See what this godly sorrow has produced in you: what earnestness, what eagerness to clear yourselves, what indignation, what alarm, what longing, what concern, what readiness to see justice done. At every point you have proved yourselves to be innocent in this matter. So even though I wrote to you, it was neither on account of the one who did the wrong nor on account of the injured party, but rather that before God you could see for yourselves how devoted to

us you are. By all this we are encouraged. (2
Corinthians 7:8–13)

Too many times our feelings of guilt lead to worldly
sorrow because of a sense of helplessness or worthlessness.
Some have described the sense as wallowing in sorrow. It
can blossom into playing the martyr seeking sympathy
and attention for being badly treated. Pride of ownership
of this need for sympathy and attention can draw one into
a false sense of hiding from God.

Can you really hide from God? You can only hide
from God in your own mind. All you are really doing is
turning your face away from God. He is still there. He still
sees you. Turning from him doesn't remove his presence.
The solution to overcoming your sorrows isn't in dwelling
in them or hiding from God. The answer is to have the
courage and faith to face God.

We have been given a path out of this sorrow if we turn
to God. We can confess our sorrow to God. Godly sorrow
brings repentance and a greater reliance on God.

> If we claim to be without sin, we deceive
> ourselves and the truth is not in us. If we
> confess our sins, he is faithful and just and
> will forgive us our sins and purify us from
> all unrighteousness. If we claim we have not
> sinned, we make him out to be a liar and his
> word is not in us. (1 John1:8–10)

YOUR THOUGHTS?

- Is there a particular instance or person that comes to mind as an example of someone given undeserved forgiveness?
- Do you agree that forgiveness and forgetting are two different things?
- What steps would you recommend to someone asking your guidance to be able to forgive someone else?
- Have you ever asked someone for forgiveness?
- Do you think that Christians have more of a duty to forgive than non-Christians?
- What do the following Biblical passages state about forgiveness?

    1 John 1:9
    Matthew 6:14,15
    Ephesians 4:31,32
    Matthew 18:21,22

🌱 12

ABOVE ALL, LOVE

🐦 LOVE DEFINED?

I can't begin to list all the ways I have defined love in my life. I had a few girlfriends in high school. I'm still not sure, but love seemed to be part of those relationships. I love to eat certain foods and do certain things. But those change over time.

I have had a few friends whose relationships were especially important to me. Love my wife. That's a big one. Found a whole new dimension of love with our daughter. And God's love, that's beyond comprehension.

I'm not sure something as big as love can be defined in a worldly context. Maybe we are limited to providing examples of love or only defining pieces of it. I do know that love is sought to find purpose and fulfillment. And without love, nothing has a real sense of value.

I suppose God knows we have our limitations with something as universal and foundational as love. After all, God is love, and we surely are limited in our understanding of him.

God has patience, and although I can't find a biblical

verse that directly supports it, he must have a keen sense of humor when it comes to our childlike efforts to define love. Otherwise, the frustration level must be high in heaven with all our mishandling, misrepresenting, and misunderstanding of something so precious and important as love.

❧ SOMETHING HARD TO DEFINE

At the time this material was written, an internet search for the word *love* brought up nearly three billion sites. Obviously love is a universal topic of interest. It's personal, and everyone defines it differently. Most of us are confused about love at least some time in our life. Perhaps love is our greatest emotion, desire, responsibility, and purpose all rolled up in one word. Maybe it defines our essence.

As a part of speech, we can use the word *love* as a noun or as a verb, for example, "She's the love of my life" or "I love him more every day." The word can relate to romantic, passionate feelings. It may be used to describe authentic relations as those between close friends. There's playful love, unconditional love, and love of one's self. There is committed love. Biblically, the use of the word *love* can be traced to three different words: Eros relating to romantic love, philia relating to brotherly love, and agape relating to universal love for others.

God desires to be loved. He desires all of us to be loved. He loves us. In fact, the Bible states that God is love (1 John 4:16). No wonder we can't grasp the fullness of the definition of love; love is greater than we are. We can no more easily define God in entirety.

↶ INSTRUCTED TO LOVE

God's love surpasses knowledge (Ephesians 3:19). We, however, have been given accounts of how God shows his love for us.

> For God so loved the world that he gave his one and only Son, that whoever believes in him shall not perish but have eternal life. For God did not send his Son into the world to condemn the world, but to save the world through him. (John 3:16–17)

> No one has ever seen God; but if we love one another, God lives in us and his love is made complete in us. (1 John 4:12)

It should be no surprise that we desire to love and be loved. Genesis 1:27 states that we are created in the image of God. And God is love. "And so we know and rely on the love God has for us. God is love. Whoever lives in love lives in God, and God in them" (1 John 4:16).

What fuels our ability, need, and desire to love? Simply answered, because God loved us first. "We love because He first loved us" (1 John 4:19).

↶ LIFE OVER DEATH

There is no way to write about God's love in entirety. We can only define it as the gift of Jesus's life, death, and resurrection. God's love gives us life and victory over death.

Because of the Lord's great love we are not
consumed, for his compassions never fail.
(Lamentations 3:22)

This is how God showed his love among us:
He sent his one and only Son into the world
that we might live through him. (1 John 4:9)

God gives you the freedom to pursue life over sin and
death. For example, read Romans 6 and Deuteronomy
30. This freedom leads to desire a life with purpose and
fulfillment. Romans 8 and Psalm 103 are some good
portions of scripture that relate to a desire for life. And
it follows that the joy of God's love leads to desire others
receive his love.

⮞ EXPERIENCING GOD'S LOVE

We are given many insights into God's love and his desire
for us to love in scripture. First, love comes from God. So
to experience truthful love-based relationships, we must
know God.

Dear friends, let us love one another, for love
comes from God. Everyone who loves has
been born of God and knows God. Whoever
does not love does not know God, because
God is love. (1 John 4:7–8)

And hope does not put us to shame, because
God's love has been poured out into our

hearts through the Holy Spirit, who has been given to us. (Romans 5:5)

And for truthful, love-based relationships, we must first trust that God's love for us is real and unfailing.

The Lord loves righteousness and justice; the earth is full of his unfailing love. (Psalm 33:5)

Know therefore that the Lord your God is God; he is the faithful God, keeping his covenant of love to a thousand generations of those who love him and keep his commandments. (Deuteronomy 7:9)

Although expected but so unfortunate, we have taken it upon ourselves to redefine love. We tend to categorize it away from God's instruction and authority. As such, our pursuits to find love and our desires to show love are often misguided and miss the mark of fulfillment.

Being off-target may be expected because we don't fully understand the breath of God's perfect love. It is unfortunate because love founded on anything other than God is harmful to our sense of worth, well-being, and pursuit of purpose and fulfillment. Oh, but we continue to try in futility by quenching our desire with convenient substitutes often arising from boredom, loneliness, and insecurity.

We are given clear warning about the essentialness of love and accepting substitutes for God's love.

Do not love the world or anything in the world. If anyone loves the world, love for the

Father is not in them. For everything in the world—the lust of the flesh, the lust of the eyes, and the pride of life—comes not from the Father but from the world. The world and its desires pass away, but whoever does the will of God lives forever. (1 John 2:15–17)

If I speak in the tongues of men or of angels, but do not have love, I am only a resounding gong or a clanging cymbal. If I have the gift of prophecy and can fathom all mysteries and all knowledge, and if I have a faith that can move mountains, but do not have love, I am nothing. If I give all I possess to the poor and give over my body to hardship that I may boast, but do not have love, I gain nothing. (1 Corinthians 13:1–3)

Whoever loves money never has enough; whoever loves wealth is never satisfied with their income. This too is meaningless. (Ecclesiastes 5:10)

So what does real love look like? God's love is unfailing and endures forever. "For the Lord is good and his love endures forever; his faithfulness continues through all generations" (Psalm 100:5).

God loves justice and those who pursue righteousness.

For the Lord is righteous, he loves justice; the upright will see his face. (Psalm 11:7)

> The Lord detests the way of the wicked, but
> he loves those who pursue righteousness.
> (Proverbs 15:9)

And God corrects those he loves. "Those whom I love I rebuke and discipline. So be earnest and repent" (Revelation 3:19).

True love comes from a pure heart, a good conscience, and sincere faith. "The goal of this command is love, which comes from a pure heart and a good conscience and a sincere faith" (1 Timothy 1:5).

Romans 12:9–21 expands on how these virtues are expressed by instructing us to hate evil, cling to goodness, and be devoted, spiritual, joyful, patient, faithful, sharing, hospitable, harmonious, humble, forgiving, and supportive.

God has given us the freedom to experience true love. We have been given the ability and sense of purpose to experience and express love, joy, peace, forbearance, kindness, goodness, faithfulness, gentleness, and self-control.

> You, my brothers and sisters, were called
> to be free. But do not use your freedom to
> indulge the flesh; rather, serve one another
> humbly in love. For the entire law is fulfilled
> in keeping this one command: "Love your
> neighbor as yourself." (Galatians 5:13–14)

> But the fruit of the Spirit is love, joy,
> peace, forbearance, kindness, goodness,
> faithfulness, gentleness and self-control.
> Against such things there is no law. Those
> who belong to Christ Jesus have crucified the

flesh with its passions and desires. Since we live by the Spirit, let us keep in step with the Spirit. (Galatians 5:22–25)

Likely the most thought of verses about love within the Bible is found in 1 Corinthians 13.

Love is patient, love is kind. It does not envy, it does not boast, it is not proud. It does not dishonor others, it is not self-seeking, it is not easily angered, it keeps no record of wrongs. Love does not delight in evil but rejoices with the truth. It always protects, always trusts, always hopes, always perseveres. (1 Corinthians 13:4–7)

Isn't it a wonder why we are still so unsure about love with such clear descriptions?

How important is love for followers of Jesus? Love's way is excellent. Love is the essence of our gifts from God.

And yet I will show you the most excellent way. (1 Corinthians 12:31) If I speak in the tongues of men or of angels, but do not have love, I am only a resounding gong or a clanging cymbal. If I have the gift of prophecy and can fathom all mysteries and all knowledge, and if I have a faith that can move mountains, but do not have love, I am nothing. If I give all I possess to the poor and give over my body to hardship that I may boast, but do not have love, I gain nothing. (1 Corinthians 13:1–3)

God desires us to seek and express excellence. Why? God is excellent, and he wants to bless us with a life with him. God has given us a way to excellence through the death and resurrection of Jesus. And he has given us the Holy Spirit to guide us. While God has freely given us abilities that enable us to fulfill our purpose, they are nothing without love.

ᐣ WHAT'S A PERSON TO DO?

So what are we to do with this knowledge of genuine love? Again, scripture demonstrating real love is abundant throughout the Bible. Here are a few that may help in your quest for love. As you read through them, identify how you are to respond in accordance to them.

> Jesus replied: "'Love the Lord your God with all your heart and with all your soul and with all your mind.' This is the first and greatest commandment. And the second is like it: 'Love your neighbor as yourself.' All the Law and the Prophets hang on these two commandments." (Matthew 22:37–40)

> Be devoted to one another in love. Honor one another above yourselves. (Romans 12:10)

> Therefore, as God's chosen people, holy and dearly loved, clothe yourselves with compassion, kindness, humility, gentleness and patience. (Colossians 3:12)

Be completely humble and gentle; be patient, bearing with one another in love. (Ephesians 4:2)

But if anyone obeys his word, love for God is truly made complete in them. This is how we know we are in him: Whoever claims to live in him must live as Jesus did. (1 John 2:5–6)

Follow God's example, therefore, as dearly loved children and walk in the way of love, just as Christ loved us and gave himself up for us as a fragrant offering and sacrifice to God. (Ephesians 5:1–2)

In fact, this is love for God: to keep his commands. And his commands are not burdensome. (1 John 5:3)

Dear children, let us not love with words or speech but with actions and in truth. (1 John 3:18)

Do everything in love. (1 Corinthians 16:14)

Above all, love each other deeply, because love covers over a multitude of sins. (1 Peter 4:8)

YOUR THOUGHTS?

- Can you remember a particular song, story, or movie about love? What was the message?
- What words do you use to describe love?
- Describe how people view love of different entities: true love, love of life, love of food, love of parents or children, and love of their spouse.
- How do you describe a desirable relationship between best friends?
- How do you describe a desirable relationship between parents and their children?
- How do you describe a desirable relationship between those married to one another?
- How does being a Christian help define our perception of love?
- What do the following Biblical passages state about love?

    Deuteronomy 7:9
    Psalm 33:5
    1 John 2:15-17
    1 Corinthians 13:1-3
    Revelation 3:19
    1 Timothy 1:5
    Matthew 22:37-40
    1 Corinthians 16:14

🌱 13
SHARING WHAT YOU REAP

❧ GOD LOVES YOU

Several years ago, our community suffered a great tragedy. A young lady, just off work from a fast-food place, intentionally drove her car into our annual fall parade. Several lives were lost and many more seriously injured.

I remember thinking at the time that I wished I had been in the fast-food place prior so I could have helped in some way to keep her from doing such a horrific thing. My thoughts were partially fueled by compassion for her and those she hurt. There was also a sense of duty and a dose of arrogance that my efforts would have been the solution. Months afterward, I began to think about my thoughts on the tragedy. I wondered what I would have done if given the opportunity I had wished for.

Fast-forwarding several months, I walked into a fast-food place with no intention other than to use a coupon for a deal on a meal. I ordered—or should I say tried to order—noting the bad attitude of the young lady behind the registry. Little was said, and tone of what was said was not positive. I didn't mention my observation, thinking I was doing her a favor. Clearly, her attitude needed correcting.

Sitting down, I noticed her manager quickly spoke to her. The detective in me led me to believe she was upset about her work schedule. I also noticed how patient he was. He talked to her, let her talk, and then allowed her to go outside for a while before further action was taken. *Good job, manager,* I thought.

She returned; they spoke. She quickly walked to my table and asked me to forgive her rudeness. My surprise was my sense of not knowing what to do. I stated something like, *No worries,* as she reached out to shake my hand, all the while trembling. We made eye contact. I knew more needed saying.

To my surprise and dismay, all I could come up with was "God loves you." She broke into tears, reached down, hugged me, and thanked me. She quickly returned to her station, the manager still overseeing her. A customer came in, this time to be greeted with a smile.

I was in a little shock, a little surprised, and greatly humbled. I was also a little disappointed at the shallowness of my response. Surely, I was capable of more. A couple next to me said, "Man, you made her day."

I responded, "No, she made mine."

Reflecting on both instances, I learned once again that it is not about me. It is not about my talents, abilities, or best intentions. All I had done in the interim of the two events was to open myself to God and ask to be used by him. He knew what was needed. He knew my abilities. He was able to demonstrate that he was all that was needed. Anything else would not be as complete.

❧ GIFTS GIVEN

I apparently have a gift for teaching if you believe all the awards and accolades received while with the university. While appreciated, awards didn't mean much more to me than necessary for positive evaluation of work performance. It was much more important to me to just try to do my best in all situations of serving those in need of my talents.

The gift of teaching has led to opportunities beyond employment. Volunteering, sharing ideas on a variety of subjects, and interacting at church are but a few ways this gift has helped define me. This book is yet another example of my desire to teach.

Nonetheless, I often feel inadequate to share God's importance to others in everyday settings. Truthfully, I often desire to avoid such encounters. After all, who am I to represent God with all my shortcomings? What if I don't have the right things to say? What if I misspeak? Representing God is a big deal.

❧ START AND END WITH PRAYER

I continue to have feelings of doubt, which result in inaction. I continue to struggle with being proactive in sharing God's love. This struggle has led to one positive change: I pray for guidance and help. And I keep praying.

I ask that my pride doesn't interfere and that God's correction humbles me. I ask God for opportunities to share his love and message of life. And I ask for heightened awareness for opportunities, be it during planned or coincidental encounters.

He has answered. I've especially noticed many more

coincidental encounters that lead to sharing the gospel. And I am sure that more would be presented or noticed if I would spend more time in his word, more time in prayer, and more time in fellowship with other believers. "Therefore confess your sins to each other and pray for each other so that you may be healed. The prayer of a righteous person is powerful and effective" (James 5:16).

Like many, I find many distractions to occupy my time. I tend to pursue goals that don't require a large amount of energy or courage. Laziness, selfishness, and pride lead to complacency. At times I do feel led by God, as real as being physically pulled toward a direction or need. Other times, I don't feel as led. The treatment for my complacency lies within refocusing toward habits of meditating on God's word, fasting to focus on God's presence, and increasing time in fellowship. Add to those habits the essentialness of prayer.

➤ SEEKING HOT SAUCE

I mentioned a few sections ago that I am not as active in sharing God's message as I could be. I also mentioned that asking to be directed to opportunities to do so can be a powerful prayer. Maybe it results from an increased awareness of God's provision that prayer brings forth. Maybe God wants to bless me. When prayed for, opportunities to share God's purpose and love seem to arise at the oddest times.

I relate the following experience because of the impact it had on my life. I often find myself on a path without real purpose, usually preoccupied with some senseless search. To counter, I pray for God's intervention in my life and opportunities to relate who he is to others. And I am given those opportunities, even when on some senseless search.

A while back, I was on the hunt for a bottle of hot sauce. I don't remember why I thought it was so important to make a special trip to the grocery store. I had time on my hand, and what initially was a desire for the hot sauce turned into a sense of need. That quickly turned into an obsession as I made the third lap through every aisle in the store.

No matter how hard I looked, it wasn't to be found. As I was making my fourth lap, I thought to myself that I hoped the person observing my actions on the security camera passed it off as senility rather than a shoplifting suspect. I knew it was silly to continue, but compulsion to complete a task consumed my actions.

I finally gave up deciding there was no such item in the store. To save face of the waste of time spent, I decided the least I could do was buy peanut butter. We could always use more peanut butter. I knew where it was. I had passed it several times in my quest for hot sauce. As I went to pick up a jar, I noticed my access was cut off by a man standing in front of the peanut butter.

I waited. He didn't move. I continued to wait. I needed the closure that buying peanut butter would bring. He was in the way. What seemed like a half hour passed. Finally he turned around and asked, "Know anything about peanut butter? I want to get some for my wife, and I want it to be the best kind."

It was his lucky day. He was speaking to a PhD in nutrition. I gave him an oral abstract of the nutritional value of peanut butter, along with the economics of pricing.

It made me feel useful and countered the emptiness of my failure to find the hot sauce.

Then the conversation took an odd turn. He was concerned about his wife's health. According to him, she was overweight, inactive, and generally depressed. They'd been married for a long time, and from his perspective, their marriage was in as bad a shape as she was.

I listened. I offered some advice that centered on encouraging him to think of ways to improve their relationship by improving himself. This went on for several minutes, me mainly listening. I must have mentioned God somewhere in the conversation, as he confessed that they used to go to church together, but for many years, God hadn't been part of their relationship.

A conversation about God and the need for his presence in relationships followed. It ended with him asking me if I were a preacher. No, I assured him I was just a guy like him. He thanked me. I said, "No, thank God." We both grabbed a jar of peanut butter and parted ways.

I walked toward the checkout with my peanut butter. And you can believe it or not, but it is true: Glancing up at the aisle in front of the register, I found the hot sauce I had so desperately hunted.

Coincidence? Yes, it was a coincidence. Did I have a premonition that God was going to bless me in that store? No, I just was on a silly search for hot sauce. That search led to peanut butter. Peanut butter led to a man. We were both led to God.

❧ FOR THE NEEDS OF OTHERS

I carry a card in my wallet with the following prayer: Lord, I need you. Help me to trust you to meet my needs by your timing and your methods. I ask that you shape my selfish hopes, dreams, and desires so they express your will for my life. Empowered by your Spirit, I will obey you, believing as I do, in your care and love.

The card serves as a reminder to be in continual prayer with God. I know I fall short of perfection. That's ok. I know God is perfect. I also know that this relationship requires obedience and perseverance. That's also ok, for I believe God loves me.

On the back of that little card in my wallet is a list of steps that help me to organize my thoughts when opportunities to help others arise. It isn't offered as the ultimate platform that all should follow. It simply helps to direct my thoughts and actions away from my needs and toward God and others' needs. Those steps are listed below.

First, open to God's Spirit for compassion, forgiveness, and sincerity. That little prayer I provided above helps me to focus on this statement. It helps me focus on God's intention rather than my own.

Second, ask the Lord to reveal the person's true needs and for his power to meet those needs. This step requires patience and the ability to listen. Like the incidence of the hot sauce relayed, what may start out as a casual comment from someone can turn into a call for help.

Third, identify with the need of the person with mercy and compassion. This step may be particularly hard for some. I can identify. The gift of mercy is one I must continually seek. I also must remind myself to not judge or look into the past for a source of fault or blame.

Fourth, desire that they stay in the center of God's will. This, above all, is the desire for all of us. It takes the courage of faith. Courage may be in short supply in times of need and fear.

Fifth, be willing for God to use you to meet the person's need. Maybe it starts and stops with prayer and the promise to continue to pray. Perhaps it goes beyond prayer. Prayer is essential. However, God may want more from you. Prayer isn't intended to be used as a stopgap from physical giving and involvement. God may ask you to invest your time, talents, and resources to help the person. These actions require for you to have courage, compassion, and faith.

Lastly, let the person know that you will continue to pray. And do just that, continue to pray. God's actions are not on our timetable. We must get beyond the sense that if we do our part correctly, a favorable outcome will be observed in a suitable time frame of our invention. We are limited in our knowledge of God, and his ways are different from ours. Our perspectives are short-termed; God's perspective is eternal. Faithful prayer strengthens perseverance.

❧ RESPONDING TO GOD'S CALLING

Reaping the blessings of the fruit of a godly purposed life is fulfilling to a point. However, reaping what you sow doesn't end with sensing the personal pleasure of the harvest. It's the beginning. We must continually seek God's purpose for our lives to reap the harvests more fully.

Following death and resurrection, Jesus returned

to instruct and encourage his disciples. The following documents an encounter with Peter.

> When they had finished eating, Jesus said to Simon Peter, "Simon son of John, do you love me more than these?" "Yes, Lord," he said, "you know that I love you." Jesus said, "Feed my lambs." Again Jesus said, "Simon son of John, do you love me?" He answered, "Yes, Lord, you know that I love you." Jesus said, "Take care of my sheep." The third time he said to him, "Simon son of John, do you love me?" Peter was hurt because Jesus asked him the third time, "Do you love me?" He said, "Lord, you know all things; you know that I love you." Jesus said, "Feed my sheep. Very truly I tell you, when you were younger you dressed yourself and went where you wanted; but when you are old you will stretch out your hands, and someone else will dress you and lead you where you do not want to go." Jesus said this to indicate the kind of death by which Peter would glorify God. Then he said to him, "Follow me!" (John 21:15–22)

Feed my lambs. Take care of my sheep. Feed my sheep. Follow me. Jesus desires us to do as he did, to glorify God and share the good news that all can receive him through Jesus. "So how?" you ask. Our motivation must be from our love for Jesus, and we must have the courage to ask God for opportunities. And we must invest time with him in prayer, fellowship, and his word to equip ourselves.

❧ USING OUR GIFTS

Many different people and organizations have developed training with step-by-step instruction on how one can share testament of their salvation experience and the good news of Jesus. It helps to receive training on ways others have shared God's message. However, we have been given talents and abilities. Aligning our gifts with the intended purpose of the gifts will help us to do as Jesus asks.

> For just as each of us has one body with many members, and these members do not all have the same function, so in Christ we, though many, form one body, and each member belongs to all the others. We have different gifts, according to the grace given to each of us. If your gift is prophesying, then prophesy in accordance with your faith; if it is serving, then serve; if it is teaching, then teach; if it is to encourage, then give encouragement; if it is giving, then give generously; if it is to lead, do it diligently; if it is to show mercy, do it cheerfully. (Romans 12:4–8)
>
> So Christ himself gave the apostles, the prophets, the evangelists, the pastors and teachers, to equip his people for works of service, so that the body of Christ may be built up until we all reach unity in the faith and in the knowledge of the Son of God and become mature, attaining to the whole measure of the fullness of Christ. (Ephesians 4:11–13)

Your actions may center on one activity related to your gifts for lifelong involvement in ministry. They may be more diverse and most often used in social projects that benefit your neighbors. They may be more sporadic and are used more on a one-on-one basis of friendship. They may be evidenced by all the above.

Be assured you will become aware of opportunities if you invest yourself to God's purpose. Some of us may impact many people. Others may reach a few. Numbers aren't the goal; being used by God for his purpose is. Do so and you will find personal purpose and fulfillment. Do so and you will find joy and happiness.

YOUR THOUGHTS?

- What is the difference between religious practice and personal relationship with God?
- If already a Christian, have you ever shared your experience of being received by God through Jesus?
- Do you believe you have been given special and unique talents from God?
- Have you studied God's word for growth in knowing God?
- Do you routinely pray for God's direction and help?
- Have you ever discussed your search for God's love with friends?
- Do you believe that God loves you? Do you love God?
- In your own words, what do the following Biblical passages allow about sharing God's love?

    John 21:15-22
    Romans 12:4-8
    James 5:16

EPILOGUE
SOw WHAT

The title of this book was an intentional play on words. We truly reap what we sow. The question needing an answer is, "Sow what?" I hope the reader's response is a desire to sow right to God. God's desire is for your destination to be eternally with him. And God wants you to reap his blessings along the way to your destination. You will find those blessings to be so right when you sow right.

He has provided a way. Jesus came to earth as God personified. He ministered for the salvation of all mankind. He gave his life so all may have a life with God. He overcame the curse of death and, in doing so, offers the gift of eternal life with him. And his desire is for you to follow him by showing others that God loves them too!

My advice? Stop what you are chasing. Focus on your relationship with God. Get close to God. Meditate on his word. Pray. Fellowship with Christians. Let him love you. Love him. Be blessed. His blessings will bring you happiness and joy. That joy will overflow to others. You desire a purposeful, fulfilled life? You will find the way is through him.

All have been given the freedom to choose: reap a life

of fulfillment by living out your given purpose with God or reap a death of emptiness by refusing God's gift and purpose. The choice has been given to mankind throughout the ages. Important? Yes, eternally important.

> Now what I am commanding you today is not too difficult for you or beyond your reach. It is not up in heaven, so that you have to ask, "Who will ascend into heaven to get it and proclaim it to us so we may obey it?" Nor is it beyond the sea, so that you have to ask, "Who will cross the sea to get it and proclaim it to us so we may obey it?" No, the word is very near you; it is in your mouth and in your heart so you may obey it.
>
> See, I set before you today life and prosperity, death and destruction. For I command you today to love the Lord your God, to walk in obedience to him, and to keep his commands, decrees and laws; then you will live and increase, and the Lord your God will bless you in the land you are entering to possess.
>
> But if your heart turns away and you are not obedient, and if you are drawn away to bow down to other gods and worship them, I declare to you this day that you will certainly be destroyed. You will not live long in the land you are crossing the Jordan to enter and possess.

This day I call the heavens and the earth as witnesses against you that I have set before you life and death, blessings and curses. Now choose life, so that you and your children may live and that you may love the Lord your God, listen to his voice, and hold fast to him. For the Lord is your life, and he will give you many years in the land he swore to give to your fathers, Abraham, Isaac and Jacob. (Deuteronomy 30:11–20)

I thank God and hope this book might in any way, at any level, help even one person to choose life. Jesus provides the way.

SOw Right

Printed in the United States
by Baker & Taylor Publisher Services